# *Practice to Believe*

---

*S.N.Arly*

# *Copyright*

Practice to Believe: A collection of magical works

ISBN: 978-0-9913209-2-9

Cover designed by S.N.Arly

Author photo by Luke McGuff, 2011 Wiscon Photobooth

# *Acknowledgments*

I'd like to thank my fabulous husband Steve for helping protect my writing time, and my children Beren and Ranna who understand far better than I could have expected, how important writing is to me. I hope I am as supportive of your interests and pursuits as you are of mine.

I have relied on the encouragement and constructive feedback from other writers to improve and grow. Without their help, I would not have identified my own weaknesses or found ways to expand my range. I remain grateful to the members of Guts and Rocks, past and present (Kelly McCullough, Anne Waltz, Stephanie Zvan, Katie Ferreira, Dana Baird and Katya Reiman), and members of Pengames (Hilary Moon Murphy, Katya Reimann, Beth Hynes-Ciernia, Linda Lounsbury, and Qat Orkin Oskow), for taking the time to give me honest and useful critiques. I am appreciative of M.H. Bonham's decision to include me in my first widely available anthology. Thanks, also, to Eric Heideman, editor of *Tales of the Unanticipated*, for his feedback on many stories, over many years. Even when I was new to the submission process, and my writing was far rougher, he treated me with respect, and made me think that I could actually become the writer I wanted to be.

# *Table of Contents*

## *Autumn*

It was quiet in the big woods these days. From atop her great pine, Zenza could see over most of her neighboring trees. Holding two branches for support, she leaned out, closed her eyes, and took a deep breath. She smiled as fallen leaves, wet from a recent rain, filled her senses.

"Don't do it!"

The horrified shout broke her out of her reverie, and she looked around for the source.

"For the love of maple sugar, don't do it!"

She knew that voice. She looked down into a young maple that had barely begun to change color despite the season. Darja stood on one of the uppermost branches and, even from the distance, Zenza could see fear on the girl's face.

"Oh, Zenza, it's only autumn."

"What are you talking about?" Why did she always have to get the nervous neophytes?

"It's not worth killing yourself," Darja said gently. "You'd be missed far too much."

Zenza rolled her eyes. "Darja, hasn't anyone ever told you that dryads can't fall to their death?" Apparently not, she realized when the girl's expression changed to one of surprise. No wonder she'd had trouble with heights once her tree reached a reasonable size. Gripping her branches more tightly, Zenza pulled herself back and quickly climbed down to a branch level with Darja's. The maple would never reach the stature of her great and beautiful pine, few trees ever did. She'd learned to be accommodating in associating with her neighbors. When you lived as long as a tree, such things made sense.

"Are you sure?" Darja asked uncertainly.

Zenza smiled when she could have taken offense. She was willing to ignore the young one's skepticism for now. "I have been around the forest a time or two."

Darja blushed with embarrassment. "Oh, of course you have... I didn't mean... I'm so sorry."

"Do try to think before you speak, dear. A polite dryad will get a lot farther with those of us who've been here a while." She stretched, letting the pine needles caress her skin, the same beautiful brown as the bark of her tree. "And what are you still doing up?" The young dryad's honey colored hair hadn't begun to change tone, which meant she hadn't even started preparing her maple for the long sleep.

"I wanted to see autumn." She lifted her chin in a defiant pose. "I've been hearing about it for years and have never seen it."

"Your kind aren't meant to see autumn but once. You know that." She let an edge of authority creep into her voice.

"Everybody else is doing it," Darja complained. She gestured expansively toward the forest, where there were other trees whose leaves had barely begun to turn.

"Red maples are notorious for cutting it close," Zenza said, disregarding many of the unchanged trees. "Their leaves rarely change, and they hold on to many of them until the first snowfall." She quickly swung down to the next branch. "Come with me, I want to show you something." Her bare feet hit the ground so lightly they hardly made a sound. Dryads were naturally able to walk through dry leaves and pine needles without making much noise. Some were better than others, and she was proud of her silent step. It had taken decades to perfect, but was well worth the effort. She'd been able to sneak up on more than one man that way, and by the time they saw her, she'd already woven her magic around them.

Darja dropped down out of her tree, making considerably more noise. She patted the sugar maple's trunk before approaching Zenza. "What is it?"

Zenza grabbed the younger one's hand and pulled her through the woods. "If I told you, it wouldn't be a surprise."

Darja squealed in delight. "I love surprises!"

Zenza grinned at her. "All dryads do." The trees swayed in the gentle breeze, sending leaves in varied shades of red, gold, and rust spiraling down to the forest floor. It was her favorite time of year to run through the forest. So many dryads were already into the deep sleep, and many others were preparing their trees for the cold to come. As an older, wiser dryad, Zenza kept her tree ready most of the time. And she managed to do it without missing a single party.

The deciduous dryads often complained about not getting to see the splendid autumn colors that her kind was privy to. Zenza had always believed in balance, and she suspected that autumn was compensation to her kind for the disrupted winter sleep they endured. Winter was not necessarily a joy to be awake through, although it also had its advantages. Perhaps if the weather was right this year, she could catch a man for solstice. What a lovely gift to her tree.

Darja's hand was clammy despite their exercise. "Are you all right?" Zenza slowed down and looked at her companion.

Darja nodded. "I didn't realize how cool it gets this time of year."

"Autumn's the transition to winter, which is cold enough to kill. Of course it's chilly now." They were nearly to the place.

"Do you have many parties in the winter?"

Zenza laughed. "Afraid you're missing out on the fun while you sleep?"

Darja blushed but didn't answer.

"We're dryads, of course we have parties. They're not as big as the summer parties, and we don't have them as often." She wouldn't mention the dancing or the songs to the winter stars. Darja didn't need anything else to add to her indecision about the deep sleep. "We'd get pretty lonely if it weren't for the parties and occasional travelers."

"Humans travel in the winter?"

Zenza giggled. "They're not like us. They can't sleep through the winter. They'd starve."

"Really?"

"Ever seen a human?"

"Well yes," Darja said quickly. "They look a lot like us."

"But they age," Zenza said. "And they have such short lives." She'd stopped counting the years at 300. Appearance was irrelevant when gauging a dryad's age. It was all in the attitude, which seemed to grow as the trees did.

"They get old?"

"Quite rapidly," she agreed. "You know there are two kinds of humans, men and women?" At Darja's nod she continued. "The women are a little like us." She ran one hand down the side of her body, emphasizing the swell of her breasts and curve of her hips. "The men make good lovers, though you've got to catch them first." She grinned in delight. Men were almost as fun as parties.

Darja froze and tried to pull her hand away. "Are you crazy?"

"You've got tree-love," Zenza replied with a laugh.

"Don't you love your tree?" Darja looked horrified, as if Zenza's words were blasphemy.

"Of course I do," Zenza said. "But I'm not blinded by his beauty anymore. We all go through it, so don't think I'm teasing you." She squeezed the younger one's hand. "But when you grow beyond that, you'll see that there are many ways to help your tree."

"Doesn't he get jealous?"

It took all her effort not to laugh out loud at the girl. "Oh goodness no. He likes anything that makes me happy. Besides," she continued with a shrug. "With no other pines nearby it's one of the few ways for us to propagate."

Darja just stared, her face a mixture of horror and awe. She'd evidently never been told this either.

"You won't be interested in humans for a while, I think," Zenza said gently. "But believe me, they can be very nice."

"But aren't they dangerous?" Darja whispered. "I've heard they kill."

She sighed. "Sometimes they do. And some are very dangerous." In her youth, several dryads had been captured and taken away by humans. They must have been treated quite badly, although they clearly weren't killed outright. The tree was the reflection of the dryad, and the reverse was also true. One could not survive if the other died. Those trees had languished for years with no one to care for them. Zenza had been required to cut one tree down to end his suffering. It killed his lost one wherever she'd ended up, and he wanted to end her misery. It had been very difficult, but a dryad couldn't refuse a tree's request, even if it wasn't her own. She shoved the memory back down where it had come from.

"I only go after the ones who travel alone, and I always bind them first. Our magic works well on humans." Zenza tugged on Darja's hand to get her moving again. "We're almost there." She tightened her grip all but hauling the young dryad into the grove. "Here we are."

Darja shrieked and tried to pull away.

"Oh, now stop that!" Zenza snapped. Young ones were so flighty and quick to panic, but this was a lesson she needed to learn if she wanted her tree to live to fifty.

Scattered about the grove were a number of maples, all stunted and badly damaged. Great sections of the trees were dead, while other parts continued to live. Dead branches hung loosely by the fibers of the bark. Others rotted in their original positions on the tree, as if the dryads had been unable to perform appropriate maintenance to remove them.

"Zenza, take me home!" Darja wailed as she slapped at the older dryad's hand.

Zenza grabbed the scruff of the girl's neck and gave her a shake. "I'm your elder and you will behave yourself." She released Darja once she stopped struggling. "This is very important, and you'd do best to pay attention."

"This is a terrible sickly place," Darja whimpered. "What happened?"

"Nine years ago the dryads of this grove decided they needed to see the leaves change." She pulled Darja over to the nearest tree and gently lay her free hand on the trunk. "It takes time to prepare a tree for the deep sleep, and they waited too long. The frost came hard, and the dryads were hurt as much as their trees. Some died outright." She glanced over her shoulder to one of the unlucky ones. Or perhaps it was lucky to have been spared this continued misery.

"But some lived," Darja said quickly. "These trees are still alive."

"Yes, some lived."

"Why don't they take care of their trees then?"

She met the girl's eyes. "How well could you trim your tree's damaged limbs with only half your fingers or one hand?" She let go of Darja's hand, certain she wouldn't bolt now. "They do the best they can, and for the stronger ones there will eventually be recovery, but the scars will always be there."

Darja sniffled. "Why doesn't anyone help them?"

"Some of us do," Zenza said with a nod. "But there are others who feel it is not their job to look after foolish dryads who make decisions that threaten their trees." She turned and climbed one of the damaged trees. She reached into a hollow of a dead branch and pulled out a bit of honeycomb. She dropped to the ground and held the sweeting out to Darja. All sugar maple dryads loved sweet things. The sweeter the sap, the happier the tree, the more vibrant the leaves would be.

"Oh, I couldn't take their honey." Holding up both hands, she shook her head.

"It's all right, really. I put the bees there last spring so they would always have sweet things nearby." She put the honeycomb in the younger girl's hand. "Besides, these dryads have all gone to sleep for the winter, and honey doesn't last long in the forest."

Darja nibbled at the honeycomb as she continued to look around. "I should get back," she said after a long pause. "I've so much to do."

"Yes, you have." She turned to guide the younger one out of

the grove. "I'm sorry if it upset you, but this is something we all need to face sometime."

"You're right of course."  They walked in silence a few moments.  "Thank you."

Zenza turned to her and smiled.  "If I won't teach you, what good am I as an elder?"

*Practice to Believe*

## Der Erlkönig

Long ago the Earth was more wild, and the forest of the world held great power over humankind. The face of the world has changed, but some of this remains true.

In the shadows of Schwartzwald, the Black Forest, lived a powerful king known as Erlkönig, King of Alder. He stood over seven feet in height and was easily as majestic as any tree in his domain. His robe was the blue-gray color of mist. On his head he wore a crown of leaves, of a kind never found on any tree, perpetually held in the bright tints of autumn. He carried a staff as tall as himself, and although it could have been an imposing weapon, it was never needed. Erlkönig was one of the fair folk, and while human children saw a grand figure, their parents could see only an old gray willow, battered by the elements.

Alone in his vast forest, Erlkönig might have become quite lonely. Spotted woodpeckers, red deer, and badgers could participate in conversation on only a limited number of subjects, even such creatures as have been surrounded by magic. Foxes served him by choice rather than fear or obligation. Of humankind, the children were the most like him. They alone could laugh with

9

abandon, and found pleasure in the simplest of things. Alas that human children grew up and took on the world's troubles as responsibilities, extinguishing the spark within and blinding their eyes to his visage. It was the tragic fate of the human born. Their lives were short, and they lost all joy in the world so quickly. But he had a solution.

When a boy entered the forest with his father, Erlkönig knew. When a girl child traveled the narrow roadway, he was aware. He decreed that children trespassing within the bounds of Schwartzwald between dusk and dawn would never leave. The red fox carried the proclamation to all ends of the forest, but humans were ignorant of the true language of the wild.

When a child came under the shadow of the mighty trees, Erlkönig visited as soon as night fell. Perhaps it was unfair. No child could refuse him, and they rarely even considered it. Most quickly forgot to fear him as a stranger, ran into his arms without question, and never looked back. He was more handsome than anyone they had ever seen, and they could not turn away once he had caught their eyes. His gentle voice coaxed like the fairest music. Sometimes he sang, other times he lured them with promises of all the marvelous things they would do together. He did not lie.

In his forest, where he was strongest, around those he loved the most, his power enabled him to bind the vital essence of the child, forsaking his or her first form to become one of his own; fey children who would never have to understand the weeping of the world.

* * *

"Who rides through my forest so late this night?" Erlkönig asked as he stood at the edge of the well-traveled dirt road. He could hear the pounding of a single horse's hooves, though it was still a great distance off.

"It is a father with his son," the red fox whispered. "He holds the boy close to keep him warm." He smiled up at the Lord of the Wood. "How considerate of him to pass through so close to winter, when few choose to travel with their kits."

Erlkönig bent and caressed the fox behind the ear. "How right you are." He straightened and stepped into the road, gathering

10

his glamour about him like a cloak. The rider and his precious burden approached. Closer and closer they came. Erlkönig saw the travelers long before they could see him. To the father he was little more than a shadowy cloud of fog, haziness in a low spot under the trees. The horse slowed, then shied, keeping to the far edge of the path.

The boy let out a faint gasp of surprise, and turned his head to watch as they passed Erlkönig. His mouth was open, but no words came out. His round cheeks were pink from the wind and chill. His hat and scarf were free of threads and snags, suggesting that they could not be mere cast offs from an older sibling. In an age when most children went unshod, fine leather boots were visible under his blanket wrappings. He was a treasure, cradled in the arms of the man.

Erlkönig smiled. "You lovely child, come away with me," he whispered. In Schwartzwald his voice carried to the ears of all children, be they near or far, if he wished it. "Many are the games I will play with you."

The horse continued down the road, and the father forcefully turned the boy's head to face front. The child became restless, squirming in his father's grip. It was a common reaction when someone tried to hide Erlkönig from a child who had already seen him. Such young ones were already smitten, enthralled by the king who spoke so kindly and looked so beautiful.

On swift feet Erlkönig moved ahead of the horse and riders, and again waited for their approach. In his forest he could move wherever he wished as quickly as necessary. He was not bound by the rules that restricted humans. His eyes were keen, and he could see the boy thrashing, half-hidden beneath his father's cloak.

"I will show you many colorful flowers, and dress you in golden raiment," he said. The child saw him then, and stopped struggling. Erlkönig held his staff in his right hand and reached out with the left. It was important to him that the child came willingly, despite the fact that there was no choice. He did not intend to harm the boy with force, and fear was hurt enough to grieve Erlkönig. He worked his magic patiently, knowing he had all the time he needed.

Again, the horse spooked, sidling away as he came near.

"Father?" the boy whispered in confusion as he leaned out to touch his hand to Erlkönig's. The human child went limp in his blood father's arms, his body quickly going cold. When the man checked, he would find his son dead. But standing in the middle of the road, holding the hand of Erlkönig was the same boy, turned fey. There was a healthy pale blue glow to his plump cheeks, and the light in his black eyes was brighter than it had been when they were hazel and he was yet a human child.

"Father?" the boy asked, reaching out with his free hand to grasp Erlkönig's robe. "Were you calling me?"

"It's late," Erlkönig said gently. He raised the end of his staff to the sky. "The moon will soon take flight, and we've hardly had the chance to play." Hand in hand they walked into the woods. "Let us leap to and fro, merry as we dance our way home."

The boy laughed with delight and slipped loose to run ahead, free. Like a deer, he bounded over fallen trees and low-lying dips, spinning when he landed, and giggling when he fell into a pile of leaves and pine needles.

"Are you happy?" Erlkönig asked, easily keeping pace.

"Oh yes," the child replied as his feet splashed through a puddle so small that it could scarcely bathe a star. He paused and stared at Erlkönig. "I love you, father."

Erlkönig smiled. "And I love you, my stolen child."

\* \* \*

The mother was bereft. She knelt beside the body of her daughter and howled, an almost inhuman sound of unmeasurable suffering. Again, she grasped the prone child's shoulders and shook her, begging her to wake. Her words were inarticulate and frantic, uttered in the desperation of one who knew it was too late. Holding the cold girl to her breast, the woman turned from despair to rage. She tipped her head back and shrieked her promises of revenge into the treetops.

Erlkönig was beyond her ability to curse.

He turned away from the road, following after the flighty child he had stolen. In sparing her the impoverished life she was destined to lead, he had done what was best for her, and that was what mattered. She would know no sorrow, and he would derive great joy from her happiness and freedom.

\* \* \*

Over the decades and centuries, Erlkönig's family grew. Visitors to Schwartzwald heard the echoing laughter of children high in the tops of the trees. The sound was faint, as if far away, yet the voices were clear and undistorted over the distance. Some said the forest was haunted, and others claimed it was bad luck. Others still, perhaps guided by some extra sense or exceptional wisdom, insisted it was a holy place not meant for the likes of humans.

Villages grew and expanded, cutting down more of the forest and splitting it, first in two, then four, shrinking woodlands, separate entities that were one in spirit. The roadways were widened and covered with gravel. A pungent black surface followed. Carriages were replaced with motor cars made with the death metal Erlkönig couldn't penetrate or approach, even in his own domain. They spewed noxious fumes into the once pristine air. Many of the trees, his meek and defenseless children, grew sick. The animals became fewer. But Erlkönig refused to let his children suffer or worry because their playground had become smaller. He grew faery rings, allowing them to jump to the amputated portions of old Schwartzwald without nearing the dangerous roadways.

Over time, the tales of the haunted forest and the children who died there dropped into the realm of legend. Parents grew careless. Cars occasionally broke down, leaving the passengers stranded in the dark night. Boys and girls wandered off, looking for a convenient place to relieve their bladders, or simply meandering out of boredom. Away from the cold iron they could hear Erlkönig's voice and see him in all his glory.

Then the forest stopped shrinking, and the air improved. It seemed that humans had discovered the folly in destroying everything that inconvenienced them, whether or not they understood it. While this made his home a safer place, Schwartzwald had been forever changed. Although some humans were more enlightened than those the Erlkönig first encountered, as a whole their progress was minimal. Many held little pleasure in the world or in their short lives. It seemed the world was a more tearful place than ever before. There were countless tragedies, crimes, and

13

miseries, and upon reaching a certain maturity, humans were destined to accept guilt and responsibility for things they had no control over. They lost the spark that made life worth living. He would spare them all, if he could, but his power was bound to the forest and did not extend beyond the shadow of the trees.

* * *

The girl sat, unmoving, on a half-rotten log. Her father, a bare score paces away, was swearing from underneath the hood of his vile motor car. He offered periodic apologies and reassurances that they would soon be on their way, before turning back to the machinery that had failed him so completely.

She couldn't have been more than ten, yet her expression was oddly adult. Exasperation mixed with the effort to control her temper. The fingers of one hand explored the cracks in the log. "It's all right," she called back to her father. "We'll just have to be late."

"I think she's ready to cry," the red fox said, then shook her head. "She's all dressed up for a party. Look at those ribbons in her hair. And she's accustomed to disappointment. You can see it." She turned away. "I can't stand it. I'm going home to my kits."

Erlkönig brushed her tail with a finger as she fled. She'd become quite sensitive in their association, and understood his plight better than any of her predecessors. He watched the girl a little longer, puzzled by her ability to stay so still. She didn't address her father again, although she occasionally turned her head, ever so slightly, pointing an ear in his direction. Then the Lord of the Wood realized her luminous gray eyes never moved, and he understood. He hoped it wasn't too late; that she hadn't already taken on too many burdens as a result of her blindness.

"Come away my child," he whispered, relieved when her face turned in his direction. "Come to the wild."

She looked both puzzled and awed, as she stared at him. Two small hands came up to cover her mouth.

She could see him.

He smiled, but took only the smallest step closer. "My fine girl, will you come away with me? My daughters await your arrival with great anticipation. Together, you will dance and sing."

She turned toward her father, then back to Erlkönig.

Because she saw him with pure sight, not human vision, he was the only thing she would see until she abandoned her imperfect physical form. Her beautiful face showed confusion. She frowned.

Never had one hesitated so. She was so near to losing her spark that she could consider her options and choose. "I love you, my child," he whispered. He had to convince her, to save her from the fate her kind faced. While he knew he could use force, make her stay, the very idea repulsed him. "I wish for you to walk Schwartzwald at my side."

As she gazed at him, her expression turned wistful. Finally, she stood and took clumsy steps in his direction. She held her arms out in front of her, as if expecting to run into something, as if disbelieving the one thing her eyes had ever shown her.

"Carefully, my dear," he cautioned. She stepped in a hole and lurched forward. He caught her hands on the way down, pulling her gently from her human body.

She stared at him a moment longer before discovering she could now see everything around her. She flung her arms around his neck, burying her face in his silvery robe. She trembled and would not let go.

He carried her deeper into the forest, away from the road, and soon she calmed. They sat together on the damp earth of the forest floor, and she couldn't stop looking about, running her fingers over the things she could now see. At last, her eyes settled on Erlkönig. "What have I done to deserve this gift?" she asked, her voice no more than a whisper.

"You came to me," he said, patting her hand. "It is the only way I could have done it."

The red fox and her four young kits scampered by, and the girl smiled. "Everything's so beautiful. Especially you, father." She looked at him again.

"Everything within my kingdom is wondrous fair," he said as his long fingers tucked the black strands of hair behind her ears. "And you are in my kingdom."

She blushed, her cheeks momentarily going a brighter blue, then her dark eyes went wide. "But I don't even know what I look like."

Erlkönig smiled and stood, holding one hand down to her. "We can find a pond for you to admire your reflection, and I assure you, you will be pleased."

Together they walked through Schwartzwald, gathering his other children in a large entourage. "I love you, my father," the girl said.

"And I love you," he said. "I love all my stolen children."

She looked straight at him. "Yes. But you will love me best."

\* \* \*

Humankind has dominion over much of the Earth, but the forest still has power over it. For Erlkönig of Schwartzwald is not unique to the forest of the world, and some of his kin have less kindly motives. The end of this story is unknown, and only time will determine who will live happily ever after.

### *First We Practice to Believe*

The voices were muffled, as if the two men were behind a
security glass window. They were talking about princesses, finding
a wife, and something that was very beautiful. She was so tired, and
too comfortable to really care what they were doing. Suddenly,
fresh air wafted over her. It was cool and moist, like the woods in
autumn. Although she could hear the men better, she couldn't bring
herself to open her eyes. She'd been dreaming before they came
along, she couldn't remember what, just that it had been so pleasant.

"I think you ought to kiss her," suggested the deeper voice.
"That's a surefire way to break this kind of spell."

There was a moment of silence. "Must I? You're better at
these things. Why don't you kiss her?"

"If I do, she just might marry me, and you're the one who
needs a wife," came the reply.

Fingers touched her cheek, and she realized that she hadn't
felt anything in a long time.

"She's cold," the second man said, sounding surprised.

"Of course she's cold," said the man with the low voice.

"Would you just kiss her?"

Warm lips touched hers, feather light at first, then more firmly. Life flowed through her, starting with her lips and spreading through her face and neck, gradually reaching out to revive her entire body. She took a breath, realizing she hadn't done that for a long time either, and opened her eyes. She found herself staring into the face of a young man with sandy brown hair and the most incredible green eyes she'd ever seen. As if startled by her gaze, he abruptly straightened up and nearly tripped backward over his own feet.

"It worked," he whispered, sounding awed.

"Of course it did," replied the other man. "What did you expect?"

She took another breath, delighting for a moment in the sensation of being alive. Above her spread the full branches of several trees. Her view of the sky was entirely obscured by a thick forest canopy. Some of the leaves were starting to turn. Whatever had she been thinking, sleeping in the middle of the forest? While the bed was comfortable, all quilted satins and fine silk, it was an odd place to take a nap. The green-eyed man stood beside the bed, worrying his hands together as he watched her. He looked tall, but she supposed that could have been her perspective. She was still reclined and he was definitely looming over her. He wore fine green riding leathers, which emphasized his eyes, and he had the kind of face it was hard to put an age on. He could have been as young as eighteen or as old as thirty-five. The man beside him looked to be in his late twenties. His curly dark hair had been pulled back into a neat ponytail tied with a black ribbon. He was also dressed for riding, although he wore more mellow shades of brown and burgundy. He was more classically handsome, all chiseled features and brooding eyes, but she'd never gone for that type. They too frequently had the gross misconception that they were gods.

She sat up, surprised that she didn't feel weak or tired. She had no idea how long she'd been here, how long she'd been asleep. She didn't know where she was, or even where she'd come from, but somehow that didn't bother her. She felt absolutely at home, as if she belonged here, but her memories of the past were of a far different place. She tried to recall her dreams but only ended up with a snippet of a poem recited in a child's sing-song voice. *Oh what a pallid world we leave...*

"My lady," said the man in green. "Allow me to introduce myself." He reached for one of her hands and pressed his lips to her knuckles. He kept a light hold on her fingers. "I am Prince Roric of Smaragd, land of the ruby emerald."

"Ruby emerald?" she asked, feeling lost and confused. His hand was soft and smooth, and much larger than her own. A silver signet ring adorned one long finger, and a gold ring set with red stones was its neighbor.

"Well, Smaragd *used* to be the land of the emerald," he said, "but almost twenty years ago some crazy warlock turned all our emeralds red." He shrugged. "We're still trying to find a wizard who can set things right."

"You're a prince?" She was certain she'd never met a prince before.

He smiled and straightened up proudly. "I'm *the* prince." He was nudged, none too gently, by the other man. "Oh! Allow me to present Sir Ibrihm Vejzovic."

Ibrihm bowed politely, but made no move to take her hand from the prince. "We are most pleased to make your acquaintance, my lady. How would you have us address you?"

"Oh yes," the prince said, as if it hadn't occurred to him to ask. "What's your name?"

"I'm Nadine. Nadine Watkins." She wondered if she was supposed to bow, or curtsy, or perform some other social grace she'd never learned.

The prince beamed at her, full of boyish charm. "Nadine," he said softly, as if trying out her name to see how it felt. "That's really lovely." He turned to Ibrihm. "Isn't that lovely?"

Ibrihm grinned, clearly trying not to laugh. "Quite."

The prince finally released her hand, and she pushed aside her blankets, somewhat regretfully. She swung her feet around to hang off the side of the bed, and got a good first look at her own apparel. She was wearing a dress she was certain she'd never seen before, and she wondered how she'd managed to keep it from wrinkling. The under-dress was dark blue, over which she wore a knee length hunter green tunic. Despite all the possible variants of the color, it happened to be the exact same shade the prince wore. It seemed rather simple in design, but the neckline, sleeves, and hem were stiff with detailed embroidery. An elaborately woven tapestry belt circled her waist. She wore a pair of soft green slippers. She adjusted her skirt to keep it from rumpling too much. In the process, she found a small red heart, like a birthmark, on the inside of her left wrist. She didn't remember seeing it before. She pressed it and rubbed at it, but it didn't feel any different from the rest of her skin. If it was a bruise, it didn't hurt.

She heard Ibrihm whispering to the prince. They seemed to be having some sort of disagreement.

"No time like the present," Ibrihm said finally.

Prince Roric took both her hands and knelt, somewhat awkwardly. He took a deep breath before looking up at her. "Lady Nadine," he said in a soft voice. "Would you marry me?"

She'd been asked to marry someone once before, and had said 'yes.' She later realized that it had been an enormously bad idea, and she'd left. She wasn't averse to the idea of marriage, but she'd only just met the prince. However, she couldn't quite bring herself to tell him 'no' out right. There was something about him she liked.

"I can't give you an answer," she said, unable to look away from his beautiful eyes. "I'm a little confused. I'm not entirely sure how I got here." They were in an open space beneath many large old trees. Their trunks were so thick she could have hidden herself completely behind any of them. Saplings and other young trees grew out past the old trees, as if this space were off limits to them. Out near the edge, stood two huge black horses. She didn't want to think about them just now, and she wondered if she dared hope they were a figment of her imagination.

"There's a lot I can't quite remember," she said. She could remember scenes, like pieces of a puzzle, but none of them fit together.

Oddly enough, he appeared to think that this was wonderful news. "Come back to the palace with me," he said, quickly. "We'll take care of you while you get sorted out."

She didn't think she really had any other options, though she doubted she would have turned down his offer. "Are you sure?"

He nodded, smiling up at her. "Oh yes. I would love to have you come stay with us, Lady Nadine." He stood up then, nearly falling into bed with her. His cheeks went slightly pink.

"You needn't call me lady," she said as he helped her to her feet. "Nadine is just fine."

He looked tremendously pleased. "My father would be quite annoyed if he caught me being so informal with you." He took one of the blankets from her glass coffin of a bed, folded it carefully, then draped it around her shoulders. "We can't have you getting cold," he said. "It will be chilly with the sun setting." He looked down at her feet, and noticed her slippers. "Stay here. I'll go get my horse."

"Your horse?" she asked in a frightened whisper. She'd never ridden a horse before, and she was currently as close to his horse as she wanted to get.

He smiled again. "I certainly wouldn't expect you to walk all the way back to the palace." He left her bedside to fetch the horses.

"You're the first who hasn't said 'no' right off," Ibrihm said in a low whisper. "As you've obviously never heard of him, I'll warn you now that the prince isn't terribly graceful."

She looked at Ibrihm, not sure she liked him now. "I thought you were his friend."

"I am," he said.

"Then why are you telling me this?"

"I just thought you should know." He smiled. "If he steps on your toes, it's honestly not intentional."

Perhaps he was all right after all. She'd keep an eye on him, though, until she was sure.

Prince Roric returned with the horses. "Would you ride with me, my lady?"

For all that she was worried about the horse, as well as Ibrihm's warning that the prince was clumsy, they made it to the castle without incident.

\* \* \*

21

"This is the hall of mirrors," Prince Roric said. She'd been at the palace for a week and a half, and he was finally giving her the grand tour he'd promised on their ride from the woods. "It's my mother's favorite room," he added as an afterthought.

She nodded and caught the reflection of several Nadines all nodding in unison. It was a bit disconcerting to be surrounded by mirrors in nearly every direction. The walls, where she could see them, were red, with golden ivy stenciled in the corners and up near the high ceiling. The mirrors were all shapes and sizes, and each was set in an elaborate gold frame. No two were alike. Some were very small, no larger than her hand, and others were taller than the prince himself. He'd turned out to be as tall as he'd looked when she first saw him. That was a little disappointing. He had to be looking directly at her for her to really see his eyes. She searched the room for just the right mirror; the one that would reflect his eyes. It turned out to be a small oval halfway up one wall.

"You're smiling," he said. He was wearing green, as he did just about every day. "Do you like the mirrors?"

She looked away from the oval glass, afraid he might realize what she was doing. "I don't think so," she said slowly. She didn't mind seeing her own reflection, but she preferred to see only one of herself at a time. "I feel like I'm being watched."

An expression of amused wonder lit his face. "I've always hated this room, for that very reason." Taking the hand that she'd rested on his forearm as they walked, he dropped to one knee in front of her. "Lady Nadine, would you marry me?"

She remembered now that her former husband had been far too serious. He cared more about his work than he had about her. She didn't know how she'd gotten from her world to this one, nor could she remember many details about her past. It had been a different world, that much she was sure. But this world was familiar to her as well, and she hadn't figured out what that meant. She still felt like she belonged here, but her conviction grew more tentative as she recalled more of her life, all of it elsewhere and none of it here. It was routine for betrothals to be made on a chance meeting here, but she wasn't sure she should bow to the custom. If she didn't like him so much, it would have been easier to just say 'no,' and put an end to it.

He'd spent some time with her every day. Occasionally it was only a half an hour here or there. On other days they sat for hours in front of the fire, playing a game with a dented wooden board and several dozen marbles. She genuinely enjoyed his company, and a part of her kept hoping he would kiss her again.

"I'm still trying to settle in," she said, hoping his feelings wouldn't be hurt. "Don't you think you should know about my past?"

He shrugged. "Past is done. It's not that important."

"I was married once," she said. "Won't that be a problem?"

"You're not married now, are you?"

"Most definitely not." She'd divorced her pain-in-the-butt husband, much to his surprise. She wished she could remember what happened next. How had she come to be enchanted until Prince Roric woke her with a kiss?

He smiled. "Then it's not a problem." He kissed her hand. "I can see that you need more time to adjust."

"If you don't mind."

"I don't." He stood and offered her his arm again. "Let me show you the rest of the palace. The best is yet to come."

He'd left *his* favorite room for last. As they climbed the tight winding staircase, she clung to his arm. Although she hadn't mentioned it to anyone, she was not exactly graceful herself. She also wasn't accustomed to wearing floor length dresses and climbing stairs. Today, she wore a lovely burgundy brocade. Queen Marwyn had selected it, as she had with all of Nadine's wardrobe, and it went rather nicely with the prince's green. It felt so strange to have people fussing over her. Everyone she'd met, from the king and queen to the lowliest serving girl, seemed very intent on making her happy and comfortable.

"Just a few more stairs," he said. He quickly glanced at her, then turned his eyes back to the steps. They finally came out in the center of a hexagonal room at the very top of the palace. "You can see everything from here." The cupola had half walls topped with large banks of windows. He led her to one side. "There's the forest where I found you." He smiled at her. "The leaves are turning now.

Just give it a week or two and it will be all red, orange, and gold."

She couldn't see where the forest ended. The few evergreens stuck out with bold color. She absently ran her fingers over the heart-shaped mark on her wrist. She was certain that it was lighter than it had been when she first noticed it. It was puzzling.

"And over here," he drew her toward another window, "you can see the city."

She looked out into the winding streets and low buildings, and froze. For a moment she had trouble breathing. She'd been here years ago. Not to the palace, of course, but she'd been to the city. She and Ellen, her best friend, had spent most of their childhood here. Even well into high school, they'd found time to visit the fantasy land they'd discovered. Somewhere along the way, they grew up and realized that their adventures couldn't have been more than very vivid make-believe. After that, it was as if they had closed the secret door into this world, locking it behind them. It had been years since she'd even *thought* of the place. Ellen had died in an accident just after college, leaving Nadine no one to remind her.

She realized that the little verse that had been playing over and over in her memory was the spell she and Ellen had used to get here. *Oh what a pallid world we leave...* But there had been another line, and she couldn't remember it. She'd never spent such a long period of time here, and she wondered if it *could* possibly be real. Was she dreaming? Was her real body somewhere else? She desperately didn't want it all to be some construct of her imagination. She liked Roric and Smaragd, with its peculiarly cursed emeralds.

She pressed one hand to the glass. It felt cold. Real. She looked at Prince Roric standing beside her. He seemed absolutely real. He wasn't perfect, like most fantasy or storybook men. He was clumsy and a little uncertain of himself. He was definitely not the stereotypical prince she would have imagined and created if she were in charge of this world.

"Can we go there?" she asked, pointing to the city.

He looked a little startled, then he nodded. "Pardon me for asking, but do you specifically mean you and I?"

"Of course... unless you're too busy," she said, realizing that, as a prince, he might have significant responsibilities. "I could go by myself."

"You most certainly will not," he said sternly. His cheeks went pink. "I don't think I meant that the way it sounded." His voice was apologetic. "I could never be too busy for you. And the city is a big place. You could get lost."

She was tempted to tell him that his big city was nothing compared to the place she came from, but she was touched by his concern. "Do you mean that?" she asked.

"Of course I do," he said. He pointed out the window. "Just look at it. It's huge."

She fought the urge to giggle. "No, not that part." She met his unbelievable eyes, and a delighted shiver ran down her back. *That* felt real. "You're a prince, you must have so many things demanding your attention. If you don't have time to spend with me, I'll understand."

"You are joking, aren't you?" His face was as serious as she'd ever seen it. "If you want it, I will always have time for you. Always." He touched her cheek, his big hand covering the whole side of her face.

Her stomach flipped over pleasantly, and she stared up at him, wishing he would kiss her. Either she was due a wish come true, or he was thinking the same thing. Fully aware this time, she savored the moment. It was gentle and sweet. It made her feel more alive than she'd ever been. He *had* to be real. She didn't think she could stand it if he weren't.

Someone coughed behind her, and the prince's head snapped up in surprise. He let out a sigh of relief and visibly relaxed. He was blushing again. "I really wish you wouldn't sneak up on me like that." He withdrew his hand from her cheek and took a small step back.

Nadine looked over her shoulder to see Ibrihm standing at the top of the stairs. He was leaning against the rail, grinning.

"I thought you might want to see this," Ibrihm said, holding out a roll of parchment tied with a red cord.

The prince took the parchment. As he uncurled it, he went to the window with the best light. It happened to be the window

25

farthest away.  As he read, Ibrihm approached Nadine.

"Good afternoon Sir Vejzovic," she said, managing a somewhat awkward curtsy.

"Good afternoon, Lady Nadine."  He gestured to the window. "And what do you think of our fine city?"

"It's very nice," she said.

"Am I to assume that you have accepted his offer?" he asked in a low whisper.

She shook her head.  "I need more time."

"You let him kiss you," he said, giving her a searching look. "I do hope you're not toying with him."

"Certainly not."  She'd encountered the prince's friend occasionally, and he clearly had Prince Roric's best interests at heart. "I like him," she admitted.

Ibrihm nodded, his face friendly again.  "Good.  He likes you too."

"Oh dear, I'm afraid we've missed lunch," the prince said as he tucked away the papers.  "My lady, I beg your forgiveness.  You must surely be hungry."

She smiled.  "I hadn't noticed, but now that you mention it, I am."

"Then let us go down to the kitchen and see what there is to be had," the prince suggested.  Both he and Ibrihm offered her an arm to escort her down the frightening staircase.

She tucked her hand through the prince's arm, smiling shyly as she looked up at him.  "You got me up here in one piece, I trust you to get me back down again."  As they made their way down the steps together, she wondered if he was trying harder.  He didn't seem nearly as ungainly as she'd seen him on his own.

\* \* \*

The city was a cluster of one and two-story buildings along crooked narrow roads.  Before leaving the palace, she'd firmly reminded herself that it was *not* a village, and as she didn't want to offend the prince, she'd best not refer to it as such.  A number of people escorted the carriage down from the palace, although most of them were servants and pages who had their own business to attend to.  She supposed Ibrihm had come along as a chaperone.

26

"Are you warm enough?" Roric asked, for the third time since they'd left the palace. They were walking through the streets, stopping at the places he thought might interest her.

Nadine nodded. "Oh yes. Your mother knew exactly what I needed." She never would have guessed that she could be so warm in a dress. She pulled her skirt up just enough to see her new boots. "These are wonderful. I could walk for hours."

"I do hope you're speaking metaphorically," Ibrihm said.

The prince laughed. "I thought you were able for anything my lady cared to do today."

"Not quite *anything*," Ibrihm said slyly. "Some things I shall leave for you alone." He threw Nadine a saucy wink.

Prince Roric stared at his friend, clearly shocked by his naughtiness.

"Now, now, Sir Vejzovic," Nadine said before the prince could reprimand him. "I don't think you're being fair." Being in the same room as the prince made her all warm, sometimes downright hot. Ibrihm had an uncanny knack for appearing whenever they'd gone beyond simply gazing into each other's eyes. She rather liked Prince Roric's kisses. Last night he hadn't been the least bit clumsy, and he'd ignored his friend's polite cough to finish what he was doing on his own terms. He'd asked her to marry him again, as he did every day, but she still didn't have an answer.

They entered a small silver shop on a busy corner. Knowing that everything had been made by hand, she found herself staring about in awe. The details were marvelous, much better than the machine manufactured baubles that passed for jewelry back home. She didn't dare touch anything, for fear that she might harm a masterpiece. One wall was covered with necklaces and bracelets. Another held rings and earrings. Nothing was locked under glass.

As she looked around, she rubbed her right thumb over the inside of her left wrist. The little mark was definitely fading, so perhaps it was a bruise after all. She wouldn't have been troubled by it, if it weren't so perfectly heart shaped. That made it seem too much like a sign, but of what, she couldn't guess.

"My lady?"

She looked up at the prince's voice and saw that he and

Ibrihm were at the small counter with the shopkeeper.

"I've found something for you," Prince Roric said, extending one hand to her. "Come tell me what you think."

She reached for his hand and let him pull her gently toward the counter. "You really don't have to get me anything," she said, surprised by the unexpected gift.

"But I want to," he insisted. He released her hand and gestured to the counter.

Alone on the smooth wooden surface, was a butterfly hair clasp. It was delicate silver, with inlaid stones along the edges of the wings. The slide stick had matching stones on both ends, but was smooth in the middle. She stared at it for a moment, almost afraid to touch it. She reached out and picked it up with two gentle fingers, then lay it in her hand.

"Do you like it?" Prince Roric asked. "You have such beautiful hair, and I thought you might want something new for it."

In the last several weeks she'd learned that silver showed up nicely in her hair. She still couldn't help but feel that everything she wore was loaned to her, but this was hers. Holding it carefully out of the way she flung her free arm about the prince's neck and kissed him on the cheek. Realizing what she'd done, and in public, she took a step back, blushing profusely. "Oh, I'm sorry."

"I'm not." He closed the distance between them. He took the clasp and handed it across the counter to the man without looking away from her. "Please wrap it safely," he said, clearly speaking to the shopkeeper, although his eyes never left hers. "We've still much of the day ahead of us." He smiled and took both her hands. "I do hope you're enjoying your first visit to the city."

She nodded, not trusting herself to speak.

"Perhaps we can do it again in the future." He let go of one hand to brush his thumb gently across her cheek.

"I'd like that," she said.

When the clasp had been safely bundled and tucked away in Ibrhim's large shoulder bag, they continued on their way. They were halfway down a block when she heard her name.

"Nadine?"

She couldn't possibly know anyone else in Smaragd, so she

ignored it.

"Nadine!" It was louder this time, so she turned around, which tugged on the prince's arm, getting his attention as well. She stared as a young woman in a light blue dress hurried down the street toward her. "Nadine Watkins, is that you?"

"Ellen?" she whispered. She dropped Roric's arm and took two steps before her old friend reached her. "Ellen?" She didn't look much older than she had the last time Nadine had seen her, before the crash. Her blonde hair was longer, and she wore it in a braid coiled up on her head.

"It really is you!" Ellen threw her arms about Nadine, squeezing her tightly. "I didn't think I was ever going to see you again. And when you walked past my shop, I was sure I was hallucinating. But it *is* you!"

"What are you doing here?" Nadine asked, torn between laughter and tears. She'd missed her friend terribly, but if Ellen was in Smaragd, did that mean none of it was real after all?

Ellen glanced at Nadine's escort and grinned. "I might ask the same of you."

"Oh. This is Prince Roric," Nadine said. He was handsome in his usual green.

"I'd guessed that," Ellen whispered. She dropped a perfect curtsey for the prince. "Your highness, it is a pleasure to meet you."

"And this is Sir Ibrihm Vejzovic." She watched as her friend was equally graceful in greeting the prince's trusted aide. Ellen had always been good at these sorts of things. "May I present you with my friend Ellen. We grew up together."

"I would be honored if you would step into my shop for some hot cider," Ellen said.

"Oh, could we?" Nadine asked, looking at the prince. "We haven't seen each other in years."

Prince Roric gave her a fond smile and touched her chin gently with the tip of one finger. "That's because you were asleep." He gestured for Ellen to lead the way.

"Asleep?" Ellen asked.

"I was enchanted," Nadine said. "The prince woke me. In the usual fashion." She grinned at her old friend.

29

"We have a *lot* of catching up to do." Ellen led them to her shop. "Incidentally, I'm a good-witch. I love it. It's so much better than working in a bank... there's really no comparison."

The prince and Ibrihm politely poked around in Ellen's shop, giving the two women a chance to speak with some measure of privacy.

"Are you going to marry him?" Ellen asked. They were sitting at the little table she used for palmistry.

"I'm not sure yet," she said, uncertainty creeping into her voice. "He's really sweet, and I do like him."

"I hadn't met him before," Ellen said, "but I like him. He has a nice vibe."

"And he's not nearly as clumsy as people say." She'd seen him trip on more than one occasion, but it was always from a distance. When she was with him she didn't notice it, and she felt far less awkward herself. Perhaps he only looked clumsy from afar, or he was extra careful not to crash into things with her. She glanced up to be sure the men were out of range to hear what she said next. "Ellen, how can you be here? You died."

Ellen smiled, showing her teeth. "I had the same problem when I first arrived. That's half the reason why I started learning magic. I had to understand what happened." She got a far off look on her face. "I remember the accident, and I knew I was going to die. Somehow, in that moment I recalled all the time we spent here. Faced with death, I was suddenly able to shed the disbelief that kept us out once we got older."

"What?"

"When we were kids we *believed* that this world existed, and the only way to get here is to believe." She shrugged. "Adults don't generally have that ability. Fantasy is just fantasy. It can't be real." She shook her head. "But it is."

"So this is a real world; I'm not in a coma somewhere?" Nadine asked. She wasn't sure she could take Ellen's word for it. If this was all an elaborate trick of her imagination, she could make Ellen say anything.

"It's real, all right. How long have you been here?" Ellen asked.

Nadine shrugged. "I have no idea. I felt like I'd been asleep for years. I've been at the palace nearly two months."

"And you still don't quite believe it, do you?"

"I want to." Her gaze turned toward the prince. The more she'd learned of her past, the more her doubts multiplied. Ellen's presence didn't exactly help matters, either.

"You're going to have to make a decision," Ellen said. "You can stay, or you can leave. Once you've made up your mind, you can't change it. If you leave, you can't come back. Most adults can't get here at all, not even once. But you and I were never ordinary, so we got some sort of single-use passport. If we could believe strongly enough, we could come back. Once."

"I want to stay here," Nadine said.

"Are you sure?" Ellen asked.

Nadine nodded.

"You'll have to give up every part of your old life and fully accept your new role. It's a lot of responsibility being a princess, you know," Ellen said. "And everything is real, though I don't think we realized that when we were younger. It's not perfect here, and our influence is that of a human."

"I want to stay," Nadine said with slightly less certainty. "I don't expect things to be perfect." If they were, Roric would be slightly shorter. "I want to stay."

"Then you have to find some way to believe that this is all real."

"What do you mean?" Nadine asked.

"Do you remember the verse we always used to get here?" Ellen asked.

Nadine shrugged. "I can only remember the first half."

"Of course it's the second half that really counts," Ellen said, rolling her eyes.

"Remind me?" Nadine asked.

"Oh what a pallid world we leave," Ellen whispered. "When first we practice to believe."

Nadine nodded. Now that she heard it, she was surprised she hadn't remembered it.

"The only way to choose to stay, is to believe. If you don't

31

genuinely believe, you might get sent back." Ellen's expression was bleak. "I don't know how to help you with this part. You have to do it yourself."

"How much time do I have?" She felt the stirrings of panic. Smaragd was starting to feel like home. She didn't think she wanted to live in a world without Roric, even if he wasn't perfect.

"Let me see your wrists," Ellen said. "You should have a mark... yes, here it is." Her fingertips brushed the little red heart on the underside of Nadine's wrist. "Have you noticed it fading?"

Nadine nodded. "Is that bad?"

Ellen shook her head. "It's a time keeper. When it fades completely, you have to have made up your mind. Once it's gone, if you're still here, you're here to stay."

\* \* \*

Nadine glanced at her wrist. The time keeper was definitely lighter than it had been when she looked at it before bed. She closed her eyes and whispered, "I believe, I believe, I believe," while spinning in a circle with her eyes closed. It no longer seemed silly or childish, and it was the only thing she could think of. Magic worked here, which gave her some reassurance.

It was chilly, and when she went to her window, she saw that it had snowed. The courtyard was coated in perfect fluffy whiteness, and the corners of her window were thick with frost. She pranced about on the cold floor, trying to warm up and get dressed at the same time.

She had her morning tea and hot porridge with the queen. Of late, they'd been taking breakfast in front of the fireplace in the ladies' parlor, while Marwyn shared tales of Roric's youth.

"Do you know if he'll be busy today?" Nadine asked. As his mother, and the queen, she often knew his schedule and she'd been willing to share it in the past. Just being with Roric made Nadine believe, and she needed the extra help just now. She knew she was close to the crucial point, and she was afraid she didn't have enough faith.

"You *do* like my son, don't you?" the queen asked. She sounded concerned.

"Oh yes."

"Are you trying to wear out his knees for any reason in particular, then?" Marwyn asked.

Nadine felt her face grow warm, and she shook her head. "I just have to be sure."

A serving girl came into the room, carrying a leather message tube. "Lady Nadine, Sir Vejzovic asked that I deliver this to you."

"Oh! Thank you. Thank you so much." Nadine hastily opened one end and tapped out the roll of parchment. She'd very stupidly realized, after her visit with Ellen, that she hadn't asked her friend to look for a spell to remove the ruby red curse from Smaragd's emeralds. Unable to get to the city herself, she'd asked Ibrihm to deliver a message for her. He'd been very nice about it, and promised to be sure she got the response.

"What is it?" the queen asked.

"I sent a letter to my friend in the city," Nadine said. "She's a good-witch, and I was hoping she could answer some questions." Ellen's response was two pages long. The first page was a letter. At Ibrihm's request, Ellen had performed a card reading for Nadine and the prince. Nadine was appalled by Ibrihm's impudence, but she was curious, so she read on. The result was that of true love and happiness, which Ellen insisted, with a great deal of underlining and fat exclamation points, explained why the prince no longer looked nearly so clumsy. Nadine and Roric canceled each other out, making them both more graceful. She was terribly embarrassed to think that her friend and Ibrihm had been colluding behind her back.

The second page outlined a spell Ellen had found to disenchant the emeralds. She was absolutely certain she could do it. Nadine realized that it was the exact opposite of a ritual they had performed as kids. As a girl, Nadine had decided that rubies were prettier than emeralds and wanted to change the national gem of their special fantasy land accordingly. Ellen had disagreed, so they'd flipped a coin to decide. Nadine had won the coin toss, and they simply pretended the emeralds had never been. It had never occurred to her that she might have been the one who upset the balance.

Nadine stood up so quickly she knocked over her chair, and

grinned when she realized that she was still capable of being clumsy when she wasn't with Roric. "I have to find him." She looked at the queen. "Do you have any idea where he is?"

"Who? Ibrihm?" Marwyn asked.

"No. Roric." Nadine righted the chair. "I have to find him."

"Ask the maid," she suggested. "The one who delivered the message. She should know where Ibrihm is, and he *always* knows where my son is."

"Oh thank you. Thank you." She scrambled out of the room calling after the serving girl. Nadine learned that Ibrihm had been out for a morning ride and returned with the message. He'd been going for a lot of morning rides to the city lately, and not with the prince. As she turned a corner, Nadine spotted Ibrihm at the other end of hall, just leaving the kitchens. "Ibrihm! Ibrihm, wait!" She ran down the hall, ignoring protocol entirely. "Where's Roric?"

Ibrihm's dark eyebrows went up for a moment. "The *prince* was in the library, last I saw him."

"The library?" Nadine asked, frantically looking around. "How do I get there?"

"I'll take you," he said.

"Please hurry," she said when he didn't move fast enough.

He took the steps at the end of the hall two at a time, leaving her to catch up. "What's the rush?" He led her around a corner.

"I've got good news for him." She could hardly wait to tell him. She loved to see him happy, and she wanted to be the cause. "How far is it?" she asked.

"It's right up here," Ibrihm said, sounding very calm. "Whatever has you so excited?" They reached the tall dark doors of the library. She remembered them from her tour, but she hadn't been back since. He pushed a door open, and gestured for her to enter.

"It's a surprise." The library was a large room with shelves that reached the high ceiling. "Roric," she called. Her voice echoed. "Roric are you in here?"

She heard the sound of several large books falling, then the prince came out from between two shelves at the far end of the room. "What's wrong?" His face was pale as he walked swiftly toward her.

34

She crossed the room as quickly as she could without compromising her dignity. "Nothing's wrong." She held up Ellen's letter as she approached him. "I've got news."

He glanced at the parchment, but focused on her eyes. "You called me Roric."

She was close to him now. He *was* real, and he made her feel alive. "I'm sorry. I didn't mean to offend..." he cut her off with a kiss. His arms went around her, holding her tightly. For that moment, she didn't care about anything beyond the two of them. She was exactly where she wanted to be. Then she was looking into his eyes, and she remembered the emeralds. "We found a spell to fix the emeralds," she whispered, realizing that she had dropped Ellen's letter. She couldn't bring herself to look away from him to pick it up.

"Bother with the emeralds," he said. "I love you." He lowered himself to his knees, still holding her eyes with his. "Nadine, will you please, please marry me?"

He'd taken both her hands, and she could see that the mark on her wrist was gone. Completely. She smiled, feeling giddy with relief. She didn't quite trust herself to speak, so she nodded instead.

## The Rat Catcher

"What does it mean, Mama?" Stefan asked as he walked with his mother down the winding country lane. At first glance, he seemed an unremarkable boy. He was slender, with long limbs, and he exuded a constant joyous energy. It was his eyes that gave him away. Pale blue, and intensely aware from the moment he first opened them as an infant, they were distinctly out of place in the face of a human boy.

She frowned. "It's a word for a child who hasn't got a father," she said simply.

This was a puzzling revelation. For all his youth, there were certain things he understood. He was observant, and had learned much from his surroundings. The sheep had been particularly helpful on this subject. "But I have father," he said. "I couldn't be here if I didn't."

His mother smiled in amusement. "True enough, but I wasn't married to your father when you were made. Some folks think that's wrong."

Stefan continued on in silence, his six-year-old mind abuzz with confused thoughts.

"I suppose it's time I told you about your father." She squeezed his shoulder. "If you come into the village with me, you'll hear talk. Talk is usually worth what you pay for it."

He looked up at his mother, his worldly eyes wide. This was an unexpected boon. She'd been reluctant to bring him today, as always. In the village he heard the whispers, felt the stares, but in imitation of his mother, he pretended not to notice.

"I only knew your father for a little while," she said. "He was like no man I'd ever met... because he wasn't a human man. He came from the land of Faerie." Her eyes, the very color of maple bark, stared into the distance. Though he tried, Stefan could not see what she did. "He had to go back, you see, but he promised he'd return."

"Why hasn't he?" Stefan asked, for that bothered him more than not knowing his father.

"Time moves differently in Faerie," she explained with a tolerant expression. "One day there is like years here. He'll be back for us yet." Her voice was hopeful. "Can you be patient?"

Stefan nodded, unsure what patience entailed, but eager to do it if it might bring his unknown father back.

She smiled again. "Perhaps Granddad will find you something special for being so good." After a while, she spoke again. "You favor your father. He was tall and thin, too."

"I'm not tall."

"For your age, you are," she insisted. "Your hair is curly like mine, though not as dark. But you have his face." Her fingers touched his cheek. "Especially his eyes."

Stefan decided to pay closer attention to his reflection when he next had a chance. He personally felt his mother was the prettiest of them all. She seemed young and happy while the women of the village were dour and fast to age. Perhaps that had lured his father. The fae fancied beauty, or so the stories told.

It was nearly dark when they finally spied the cottage. Granddad sat on his favorite stool just outside the front door. His hands concealed his latest project, and a small pile of curled wood shavings lay between his feet. Stefan skipped ahead of his mother. "Granddad," he called out. "We're back. Wait till you see the treasures mama got." He was especially pleased with the bright red and yellow fabrics she'd let him choose for his new clothes. They would be the finest ever, outshining even the woodpeckers and chaffinches.

In a smooth movement, Granddad stood up, left his knife on the stool, and pocketed his whittling. He took a few steps, and scooped Stefan up. "Were you good for your mother?" he asked, tweaking the boy's nose.

Stefan laughed, and for a moment the forest was as bright and sunny as midday, despite the deepening evening.

"Has he ever been aught else?" Mama asked.

"Hmm, I wonder if we have something for good little boys," Granddad pondered aloud. Gray hair was only beginning to fleck his soft brown beard and hair. "Ah, yes. I know just the thing." He carried the giggling boy into the cottage, gently setting him on his feet in front of the fireplace. As his left hand reached for something on the mantel, he winked. "Until you get good at this, I ask that you only play with it outside, maybe when you're out with the sheep."

"I promise," Stefan said quickly. He stared in amazement as Granddad held out a shiny tin whistle. He wanted to snatch the prize away, but restrained himself, taking it respectfully to cradle it in his two small hands. It was the most beautiful, most perfect thing he'd ever seen. His fingers reached the holes with ease. It seemed to have been made just for him.

"Papa, where did you get that?" Mama asked in surprise.

"The tinkers were by today," Granddad said with a shrug. "I had them fix up that kettle of yours, and I traded a few small pieces. Ash carvings, mostly."

"It's such a grand gift," she protested.

"They practically gave it to me," Granddad said. "And he deserves a few grand things."

Stefan pressed the whistle to his cheek. The tin was cool and smooth, and the little instrument felt familiar. Silently, the way he tried to speak to the sheep, he swore to practice every day so they could become great friends.

\* \* \*

As promised, Stefan practiced playing his tin whistle outside daily. Within a month he was allowed to play inside after dinner. While he was out with the sheep, he composed songs for the clouds, the trees, and even the small grassy hill where the best grazing could be done. When he played tunes that reminded him of sheep, those he was keeping wouldn't let him alone. They followed wherever he went with his whistle, nudging him with their noses, and he took to leading them out and home with a special tune. Once it was perfected, he found he could even call them from a distance. Proud of his sheep song, he showed Granddad his new trick.

Granddad stared at the row of single file sheep parading out of their shed. It was a long moment before he responded, and Stefan wondered if he'd done something wrong. "Useful," he finally said. "But I wouldn't let anyone else know what you can do. They wouldn't understand it's in your blood."

"In my blood?" Stefan asked. "You mean, because of my father?"

Granddad nodded. "Because of what he was, or is. Some folks might think it isn't natural... that you're using black magic."

Stefan's eyes went wide in alarm. "Black magic?"

Granddad shook his head. "It's not, but there's no need to make people suspicious." He smiled. "You should see what else you can charm. It may come in handy someday."

\* \* \*

By the age of fourteen, Stefan had managed to charm every creature he happened upon. He'd encouraged rabbits to take up residence behind the cottage so there was always meat to eat. He persuaded foxes to keep their distance from the warrens. He'd even chased off a wild boar, making it safe to wander without Granddad having to hunt the dangerous animal. Although it had been complicated, he'd started a hive of honey bees for his mother. His special talent made life more comfortable in the small cottage.

Years earlier, Stefan had found that he needed but a few hours of sleep. As cheerful by moonlight as he was in the sunshine, he spent much of his spare time wandering the forest regardless of the season or hour. He composed songs to the moon and stars, and the animals that came out only at night. He watched these creatures and learned from them how to pass silently through the trees. He also collected herbs for Mama's cooking, with plenty extra to sell at the market. The knowledge of plants came as readily as his skill with music. His tin whistle hung from a cord round his neck, where he could reach it quickly if he were inspired or in danger.

Stefan had given up on his father long ago, though Mama still believed. He sensed that Granddad didn't expect the faerie man to return either. Initially hurt by the rejection, Stefan now suspected his father had never intended to return, had never planned on keeping his promise.

Stefan was nearly as tall as Granddad already. He liked being able to reach things on the top shelves, and he was proud to help Granddad chop wood, but he wasn't entirely pleased with growing up. His thin fingers had become almost too wide to manage the holes on his beloved whistle. He could barely play the fast-paced song for the bees, and he was afraid they might leave without his encouragement.

On a cheerful morning late in spring, he returned from his nightly stroll with bundles of fresh herbs. Mama and Granddad were still asleep when he gathered all he was to sell or trade in the market. He cushioned Granddad's carvings in a pile of fleece at the bottom of the single wheeled barrow, piling herbs and scented sachets on top. He desperately hoped the goods would bring enough money for a new whistle when the tinkers next came to town.

He could walk much faster than he had as a child, and it no longer took much time to reach the village. He preferred arriving early, when fewer people were about. The villagers still stared and whispered when he walked by, giving him an unpleasant feeling. He wasn't sure what was being criticized. It may have been his unknown father, though that seemed far-fetched given how long it had been. It could have been that few chose to live as far in the forest as his family. He supposed it might have something to do with his unusual dress. He delighted in wearing bright shades, and as many colors as his mother could work into his clothes. Even Granddad had moved away from the plain colors most folks preferred. The fabrics were more expensive, but Stefan was careful not to put holes in his sleeves or knees.

"What are you so happy about?" the baker asked when

Stefan arrived to make the usual trade. The baker required herbs, and fresh bread would be welcome at home.

"The sun is out," Stefan said. It amazed him how grumpy villagers could be, and he wondered if it came from living among so many other people. If that were the case, he would avoid living in the village when he grew up. "The birds are singing."

The man stared at the brightly clad boy as though expecting more. "That's it? Sunshine and birds?"

Stefan smiled and nodded.

The baker shook his head and went to work placing Stefan's order on the counter.

Having completed his task quicker than ever, and with the knowledge that there might be enough money for a new whistle, Stefan wheeled his little barrow back through the village. He was thinking of a cheery tune, one that matched his state of mind, and his fingers itched to go to the whistle hanging around his neck. He passed a group of children, boys and girls about his age though he thought them younger.

"Hey, piebald," one lad called.

Stefan ignored him, though he was certain he was being addressed. He'd never spoken to the village children, only the adults, and only when needed. Something wet, and not quite solid struck him in the back, and he stopped, momentarily stunned.

"I'm talking to you, piebald," the same boy said.

Stefan twisted and saw the large splotch of mud on the back of his shirt, where his mother had pieced yellow and green together in a zigzag from the neck to the hem. He turned and looked at the group of children, their filthy-handed leader at the front. He was too appalled to think of anything to say. They had intentionally spoiled his shirt. How would he explain it when he got home?

"I hear you're fourteen," the boy said. "But you're big as a man. What's wrong with you?"

Instead of answering, Stefan simply stared at the boy, baffled beyond a response. He didn't know these children, yet they thought it acceptable to treat him so? He was annoyed, an emotion he'd rarely felt, and he was ill-prepared to deal with it.

"I asked you a question, stupid." The boy's tone was derisive and haughty. "What, can't you talk?" He shrugged. "I heard your mother's a witch. Did she cast a spell on you? Is that how you got so big?"

"Mama isn't a witch," Stefan replied at last, thinking they might leave him alone if he didn't let them cow him.

The boy glanced at his friends, and for all that Stefan had never seen an unpleasant smile before, he recognized it now. As a group, the children walked toward him. "She's a witch if I say she is."

Unconsciously, Stefan's hand went to the whistle on its cord. He felt far more threatened than he had by the boar. Not even wolves frightened him anymore.

"What do you have there?" the boy demanded. "A penny pipe? Give it to me."

Stefan's hand tightened into a protective fist. "No." The children were all around him, their chins held up and their expressions mocking as they whispered and tittered like birds. "Leave me alone." He took a step back when the boy made a swipe for the whistle. But somebody had gotten a foot behind him, and Stefan stumbled. As he fell, hands grabbed for him, pulling on his hair and his colorful shirt. He most fervently batted away those that went for his whistle. A foot struck him in the ribs, another in the back. Small fists pounded against him. After a moment, he found himself on his hands and knees, and from there he could stand up. He pushed away the kids who were closest, and he saw that his barrow had been tipped over. He scrambled to rescue it, not bothering to check and see if anything was broken.

"Run away, piebald whoreson!" shouted the boy.

Stefan whirled to face his tormentor. He'd heard that word, whore, before. He'd seen Mama's hurt response, and made sure she wasn't around when he asked Granddad what it meant. His Mama had bedded a man more wonderful than any other. He'd promised to marry her. He said he'd be back. He'd left behind a growing child he would never meet and a handful of broken promises, scattered like bread crumbs. Mama had been shamed, all for something she likely had no choice in. The faerie man had probably charmed her with more than promises.

43

Stefan clenched his teeth and glared at the boy. His light eyes flashed as if there were a lightning storm inside his head. Terrified by what he saw in that glance, the boy flinched but he couldn't move quickly enough. Stefan's adult-sized hand grasped the front of the boy's shirt, nearly lifting him off the ground. "Apologize," Stefan said in a low voice.

"I'm sorry, I'm sorry," the boy squealed. "Let me go. Let me go!"

Stefan did just that, giving the boy a shove that knocked him into his friends, some of whom fell down. He looked at each of them in turn, convincing himself they would leave him alone, before going back to his barrow. Once he was out of the village, and certain no one was following him, he relaxed. But that made him realize how sore he was. He had no memory of most of the strikes that must have reached him.

By the time he arrived at the cottage, he had no better understanding for what had happened. His mother tearfully attended his hurts, all the while questioning him. Stefan could not bear to tell her what name she'd been called.

"There's not time for it today," Granddad said with an unfamiliar scowl. "But I'll go into the village tomorrow and demand recompense. There's no cause for this."

His mother loosened the ties and helped Stefan out of his shirt. "I'll soak it, love," she said, running her fingers over the dried mud. "There's a chance it won't stain."

After she had gone out back, Granddad sat down across from Stefan. "Is there anything else you left out for your mother's sake?"

Stefan told him the final details. After a moment of silence he asked, "why did they do it?"

Granddad shrugged. "Because you're different. People can be strange about such things."

That only confused Stefan more. To comfort himself, he reached for his tin whistle, but the moment his fingers touched it, he realized something was wrong. There was a dent on the underside, halfway down the length of the instrument. Although it might still be playable, the pitch would be sour. He clutched his precious whistle in both hands and wept.

* * *

That evening, Stefan climbed the rough ladder into the loft to his bed. He'd done very little once he returned home. He'd made a brief attempt to repair his whistle earlier in the afternoon, but was afraid he would do more harm than good. He lay on his back, with his little whistle in the center of his chest. It was not only distress that kept him awake. He had a strong sense that something even worse was going to happen. As he lay awake, he listened anxiously to the forest. Mama and Granddad held a whispered conversation in the room below.

Perhaps because he was so alert, or because he was half fae, he heard the unusual sounds first. There were people in the forest, a great many of them, and they were loud, unlike the tinkers or hunters who often traveled through. He sat up, grabbing his whistle in one hand. He moved to the edge of the loft and looked down at Mama and Granddad. "Someone's coming."

Granddad's face went blank with shock. Mama wore an expression Stefan had never seen, and it took a moment for him to recognize it as fear.

"What can they want?" She glanced quickly at Granddad. "This can't be."

Granddad rose, looking resigned. "We've lived here all our lives. I thought the village more tolerant than this." He met Stefan's eyes. "I'll try to talk our way out, but we should be prepared to go." He sighed. "We'll have to leave much behind." He walked to the door, pausing as he opened it. "Pack what you can. We'll need clothing and food most of all."

Stefan tried to do as he was told, but it was difficult. He couldn't understand what was happening or why, but he felt that it was all his fault. It was hard to believe they were in danger, yet at the same time there was no denying it. He had gotten down the ladder with most of his clothes by the time the villagers had arrived. From the sound, there were more people at the cottage than he'd ever seen at one time. He could hear voices, but the words weren't always clear. Someone was angry. Granddad replied. Men and women responded with shouts and jeers. Raising his voice, Granddad asked for common sense and reason.

Mama sat frozen on a stool, her trembling hands just under her chin, as she strained to hear. Her eyes were wide, and tears ran unnoticed down her cheeks.

Granddad shouted in alarm, and Stefan heard several things hit the cottage. He ran to the door.

"I beg you not to do this," Granddad yelled. "You will surely regret it."

Stefan threw the door open, unsure what he could do but determined to help. Villagers with torches and armed with rocks were back near the road. Three big men were trying to drag Granddad toward the crowd. Stefan stepped outside just in time to see one of them strike the older man on the back of the head. He went limp.

"No!" Stefan cried, a long drawn out word that seemed to bring the bitter cold of winter to shake the trees. Without thinking about it, he raised his tin whistle to his lips, frantically building a tune for a mob. It took a moment for the music to take hold, and because of the sour notes, he struggled to keep the charm in place. He walked into the crowd itself. He forced the melody to change to something soothing and homey. The people dropped their rocks. Looking slightly dazed, they turned to wander down the road back toward the village. Stefan played until well after their torches had passed out of sight. They would not return tonight, but he could not be sure about tomorrow.

Mama was sobbing over Granddad where he lay on the ground, and Stefan ran to them. "He won't wake up," she mumbled. She had blood on her hand from cradling his head.

Stefan touched Granddad's cheek and gasped in shock as the world around him changed. He could still see things as they were, but everything was overlaid with a bright white light, making it all more vibrant. While Granddad's real eyes stayed closed, his glowing eyes opened, and Stefan suddenly knew that Granddad would never wake up.

"You must not waste time, Stefan." The words were quiet and slow, a lower pitch than Granddad's real voice. "You will not be able to keep them away forever. You must take your mother away, and protect her if you can."

Stefan's eyes stung, and he couldn't speak. It had never occurred to him that there would come a time that he wouldn't have Granddad.

"Take what you can, but don't overburden yourselves," the slow voice continued. "You'll need to move quickly."

Stefan bit his lip and nodded.

"Do whatever you must to get a new whistle, or maybe a pipe now that your hands are bigger. You're going to need it." The light around Granddad was fading. "And if you ever meet that father of yours, black his eye for me." With that, Granddad was gone.

Stefan pulled his hand away, and his vision returned to normal. He touched Granddad again, but nothing happened. He looked at his mother, across from him. She was watching him, but he couldn't be sure if she'd seen or heard anything. "He's gone." There was a pain inside his chest that he'd never felt before. He hated the villagers. If his whistle weren't so badly damaged, he thought he just might use it to cause them harm. "We have to go. They'll be back and I may not be able to charm them again." He pressed his finger against the dent. "Please, Mama. We need to get our things together."

While his mother filled the barrow with food, Stefan worked quickly to bury his grandfather. There was no time for a marker or proper ceremony, but he couldn't leave the body out for scavengers.

The sheep song was still effective, perhaps because he had worked with them the longest. He was able to tie small burdens to each of the animals, allowing them to take more. Dawn was hours away when Stefan led his mother and the small herd of sheep down the road away from the village. He had no idea where they were going, just that they had to go.

\* \* \*

Stefan and his mother traveled for more than a month. They stopped every few days to rest, more for the sake of the sheep and Mama than for Stefan himself. During these times, he sought to add to their supplies. On one such foray, he discovered a perfect green hill with a ring of white mushrooms at the top. It was a soothing place and he thought the sheep might benefit, as would his mother.

She had been so quiet, and Stefan hated to see her liveliness fade so.

At first, Mama seemed reluctant to move again so soon. It took time and effort to secure bundles to each of the sheep and gather up the possessions they'd managed to bring. When they reached the hill, however, he was sure he'd been right to insist on the change. The animals spread out, contentedly grazing. There had not been a better grazing spot in all their travels. Even Mama seemed improved, giving Stefan a small smile, the first in weeks, as she lay out their blankets on the flat top of the hill.

He left them for little while, returning with fresh water and a pheasant for dinner. With the damage to his whistle, he had to work harder to charm animals, but it was still possible. They had met no one else on the road, and at first Stefan had been content with that. He did not think Mama was ready to face strangers. With time to consider their state, he was concerned. He still needed a replacement instrument, and he had no idea where to get one. Also they couldn't roam this way forever. Living day to day could be done in the warmth of summer, but it wouldn't do come winter. They'd already had some very rainy days, and even Stefan had been miserable.

"Could we stay here a few days?" Mama asked as she peeled meat off the fine bones of the roasted bird.

After so long with thoughts only of survival, Stefan wasn't sure it was a good idea. Yet he did not wish to deny his mother anything, and the place did feel safe. "Just a few days?"

She nodded. "Its restful. I think we both need it." She smiled, though it was a rueful expression rather than one of happiness. "You may not need the rest, my son, but you'll be better off for some time of leisure."

Stefan nodded, almost relieved. It was the first suggestion she'd made since they'd set out, and he needed some time to organize a plan.

That night was clear and the stars were bright pinpoints of light in the blue-black sky. At Stefan's coaxing, the sheep had huddled close to himself and Mama, all within the ring of white mushrooms. Amazingly, none of the fungi had been stepped on during the day.

"Play me a song, Stefan," Mama asked. "One you wrote for the stars."

"It won't sound quite right," he cautioned.

"I know. I don't mind." She lay back on her blankets, looking up. "I think the sheep will not mind either. Nor the stars."

The star song was filled with notes that started sharp and strong. They were drawn out until they faded into echo. There was a coldness to the music, for stars were far away and distant even from each other. But there was also beauty and hope, since people often made wishes by the shimmering light. As Stefan played, the world began to glow, much as it had during Granddad's death. It started so faint he didn't notice it. He could see well enough in the dark, but shortly he could see as though it were midday and the skies were clear. As he continued the song, he discovered that the world around him had changed. He still sat with his mother and the sheep in a ring of mushrooms at the top of a small hill, but the forest was thicker, and there were others standing outside the circle.

He broke off in the middle of a note and jumped to his feet. Mama sat up from her blankets and looked around, the now familiar expression of fear on her face. Stefan was vaguely reassured by the fact that the strangers had not crossed into the ring. The glow had not faded, and he realized, as he peered into the perfectly beautiful faces of the others, that they could only be fae. They wore flowing robes and gowns of bold varied colors and their eyes were infinitely wise.

"We do not mean to startle you." The voice was female, and it took Stefan a moment to find the speaker. "We simply meant to see who could use one of our rings so skillfully, while playing such glorious music."

Stefan could not have guessed her age, for they all looked young and fair. Her hair appeared golden in the strange glow and she was exactly his height. She smiled, and he tentatively returned the expression. She laughed, the sound of unfettered joy.

"He's one of us," a male voice said in surprise.

"Of course he is," the woman replied. She held out her hands. "You must come with us." It sounded like a request, not an order.

Stefan glanced at his mother, her eyes wide in awe. "I can't leave Mama," he said. "Or the sheep." He had a responsibility to them as well, and he would not have gotten so far without them.

The faerie woman laughed again. "Then you must all come with us."

Stefan reached down and touched his mother's shoulder, breaking the spell over her. "Mama? I don't think they'll harm us. Do you wish to go with them?"

She nodded and got to her feet. As she and Stefan bundled their things together, the faeries took up burdens that would have gone to the sheep. When he began to follow them along the narrow path down the hill, he played the first few notes of the sheep song, and his charges all fell in line. The faeries whispered together excitedly as they watched.

"What a wonderful trick," said the woman who had spoken earlier. She looked Stefan over as they walked. "I think you're not so old as you seem. What is your name?"

He couldn't recall if it was unwise to tell his name to the fae. He knew not to eat the food, although perhaps that didn't matter. He and Mama had no home to return to. "I'm Stefan."

"I am called Rosenholz," she said with a smile. "You and your mother shall be my guests, unless there are others you wish to stay with?"

"There's no one," he said quietly. Would he and Mama be shamed here as well?

Rosenholz looked pleased. "I'm glad of that."

Beginning to feel at ease, he relaxed, and his strangely bright sight vanished. It was night here, as it had been in the human realm, and while the fae were still grand, they were less so. When he made an effort, he found he could bring his other vision.

Rosenholz's house was completely concealed behind overgrown climbing roses. Only the dark wooden door, rounded at the top, was visible among the vines and blossoms. Stefan led the sheep to the back where there was a pen just the right size. Instead of posts and branches, the fencing was made of rosebushes three feet tall and tightly grown together. A little gate secured the entrance. The faeries carried their small bundles into the house and left, with one exception. A tall man with black hair in a long braid wound with silver stood just inside the door. He waited patiently while Rosenholz settled her guests.

Stefan marveled that he'd been given a room of his own to use. He would feel a trifle lost in the large bed, although it was more comfortable than any surface he'd ever slept on. Even as he settled in, he lay contorted so he could see his hostess approach the waiting man.

"What keeps you, Lorbeer?" Rosenholz asked, her voice just above a whisper.

"The queen will wish to see him," Lorbeer replied. "You surely can not mean to make her wait."

Rosenholz smiled, and there was something mischievous in the expression. "As a matter of fact, I do mean to make her wait." She gave Lorbeer a moment to look appalled, before continuing. "Can you not see in their faces that they have traveled long? They will wish to wash before being presented to the queen. I do not think she will mind."

"You presume to know her will!" Lorbeer accused.

Rosenholz shook her head. "Be reasonable. She should be told of them, and perhaps she would like to arrange an audience as suits her. She is also busy, Lorbeer. That will give them time to rest. It is not so great a thing."

\* \* \*

By the time the queen was ready for them, Rosenholz had cleaned Stefan's clothes, leaving them nearly unwrinkled and stain free. To his embarrassment, she came into his room while he dressed.

"Where did you get such fine clothes?" she asked, her hands holding up the blue and red tunic he'd planned to wear. She seemed oblivious to his discomfort.

"Mama made them," he replied as he hastily finished buttoning his trousers.

Rosenholz looked puzzled. "But humans don't wear these colors, not like this, and not for everyday clothing." Her dress was a deep purple he'd only seen on blossoms in the forest.

Stefan shrugged. "I've always liked bright things."

Rosenholz smiled. "That's because you're fae. And you've influenced your mother." She handed him the tunic and watched while he pulled over his head. "How old are you?"

"I'll be fifteen this winter." He could see that wasn't what she expected.

"You're so young," she whispered, shaking her head. "How have you learned to do what you have? Has someone been teaching you?"

Stefan looked at the ties he was fastening so he didn't have to meet her eyes. "Granddad encouraged me, but I learn well on my own."

"Has your father taught you nothing?"

He couldn't answer right away, and his face felt warm. "I've never met him." Then Rosenholz's hands were on his cheeks, pushing his chin up.

Her eyes were pale green and ancient. "Then your father is a fool." She kissed him on the forehead and stepped back. "Come. We mustn't keep the queen waiting."

The Queen's Hall was a grove of trees twice as tall as those that had surrounded the cottage. They walked between two rows of evenly spaced trees, each guarded by a faerie man or woman, dressed in a cloth that shined like gold, even without his special sight. Seven wide stone steps led up to the platform holding the queen's throne. Small groups of petitioners or counselors, or possibly friends, were gathered below the throne. Stefan recognized Lorbeer standing on the middle step, holding a long staff and looking very official.

"Ah, treasures, treasures," said a smooth voice. The queen stood as they drew near. Her hair was light brown with highlights of red and blonde, and she wore it loose, cascading over her shoulders. Her gown of burgundy and blue puddled at her feet. The sleeves were deep green and they draped to the floor, only revealing her hands when she held them out. A man stood beside her wooden throne. Like other fae, he was taller and thinner than most humans. He had unruly light brown hair that reached his shoulders. He looked upset. "And are you the lad with the whistle?" the queen asked, her green eyes twinkling.

Stefan nodded.

"Are you aware that you're fae?" the queen asked.

Stefan nodded again.

"Enke?" The name was a whisper, spoken by the man who stood to the left of the throne.

Stefan felt his mother start beside him.

The man leaned over to speak quietly with the queen for a moment. "By all means," she said, waving the back of her hand in a permissive gesture. "I would not wish to delay the reunion. It could be entertaining." As she resumed a casual pose in her throne, the man descended the steps with a smoothly flowing stride.

He came to a stop directly in front of Stefan's mother. "Enke, is it truly you?"

The tenderness in her expression made it clear who this man was. "Fenchel," she said softly. "Why did you never return?"

Fenchel looked uncomfortable, as though he didn't want to answer that question. He took her hand, instead, gently pressing the back to his cheek.

"Stefan, this is your father." She didn't even look away from the man to make the introduction.

Stefan was immediately jealous that Fenchel could so easily take his mother's attention away from him. Thinking of all that had happened because his father had not seen fit to take care of the woman who had borne him a child, Stefan backed away.

Fenchel smiled and held out a hand. "My son, you're nearly grown."

Stefan would not take his father's hand. As he glared at the faerie man, he recalled the last thing Granddad had told him. Disgusted with Fenchel's hold over Mama and his assumption that his son must be delighted to meet him, Stefan stepped in and punched his father in the face. Mama screamed and someone grabbed Stefan from behind, dragging him back.

"We waited for you," Stefan said, his voice just below a shout. "But you never came. The villagers tried to kill us. Granddad died, and it's all your fault!" He didn't struggle; he didn't know how to fight, and he knew it.

Holding a long fingered hand over one eye, Fenchel shook

his head. "I did not intend to harm anyone," he insisted.

"You charmed mama," Stefan accused. "You made her think she loved you, and that you loved her. You broke your promise."

"Stefan, please," Mama said, finally looking at him. "I told you we had to be patient."

Rosenholz stepped in front of him, holding his face again. "You must calm down. There is much you do not know." Her eyes were sympathetic. "We fae have few children, too few. Those of us who travel into the human realm have better luck, but often we require the help of a human, and even those pairings are not always successful. Your mother will be honored, here, for what she has been able to do for Fenchel. She may well be able to bear him another child."

Disgusted, Stefan tried to pull away, but found he was held too tightly. He glanced over his shoulder and saw that it was Lorbeer who restrained him.

"Have you never wondered why we are rumored to steal children?" Rosenholz asked.

"I thought that was a lie," Stefan muttered.

Rosenholz shook her head. "It isn't. Children who are taken young enough can become like us, though not as strong or long-lived." She released him then. "You mustn't be angry with Fenchel. He was only doing what he must."

"If I let you go, will you leave your father alone?" Lorbeer asked.

Stefan nodded. "Yes. And I keep my word," he said firmly.

Lorbeer straightened Stefan's tunic before picking up the staff and returning to his post on the central step.

"The queen is not done speaking with you," Rosenholz said, taking Stefan's arm and turning him toward the throne.

The queen remained seated, and her smile was satisfied, almost smug. "I understand that your music is like magic," she said. "I wish you to play me something."

Stefan took the tin whistle in one hand. "I'm afraid it won't sound right," he said, worried that flawed music would not be welcome here. "My whistle was damaged, and I have yet to buy a new one."

The queen laughed, a happy sound that echoed through the trees. "Very well, I shall make you a bargain. Play me a song, and I shall not expect it to be perfect. If it pleases me, I shall give you a new instrument."

Stefan nodded. He could only do his best, and hope the faerie queen would be fair. He chose one of his songs for the trees, the green leafy ones since there were so many around. Full rich sounds mingled with delicate flutterings like leaves in the wind. The sliding pitch of squirrels hopping from branch to branch mixed with the two-tone chirping of birds, though he always returned to the theme of the trees. True, some of the squirrels sounded distinctly unwell and some of the leaves seemed to be falling from the branches, but it turned out better than he had any reason to expect. When he finished, the Queen's Hall was silent. He held his whistle tightly, the finger holes making dents in his skin.

At long last, the queen let out a sigh, like a gentle spring breeze. She rose from her throne and flowed down the steps to Stefan. She towered over him. "You have a powerful gift." She smiled, looking pleased. "I shall give you a suitable instrument to accompany it." Seemingly from nowhere she held out a golden pipe. "And I welcome you to our number."

\* \* \*

Stefan chose to live with Rosenholz, who turned out to be a distant cousin. She had also spent her first years outside of Faerie, which meant she often knew what his upbringing lacked. His mother had gone to the house of Fenchel, and in the last four years had been delivered of both a daughter and a son. She seemed happy, but Stefan was unsure if it was genuine. He visited weekly, most often when his father was attending the queen. He had come to tolerate Fenchel, but only just.

Stefan and Rosenholz routinely traveled the human realm together. Stefan played his golden pipe in exchange for money or things to bring back home. While animals and humans were still the easiest to control, he could now call upon the weather and plants. He ended a drought in the north and was rewarded handsomely. It had taken weeks to shepherd his new animals home to Faerie. He banished locusts and summoned deer. Although he was bent on being helpful, he felt completely useless in his cousin's search for a breedable man. She had decided she was ready for a child, and suggested that Stefan might likewise began his own search. She pointed out that he might try in Faerie first, since he'd grown up among humans and spent so much time away. Although he was willing to help her, and he found some of their people caught his attention in exactly the right way, he wasn't ready to be a parent. And he fully intended to be the sort of father Fenchel hadn't been.

They traveled once to an island country, beautiful and green, although different from home. Stefan had heard there was a plague of snakes, which seemed just the sort of thing for himself and his pipe. Unfortunately the snakes turned out to be people, vilified by a new and quickly rising religion. While he could have used his skill against them, it was a human struggle and not the sort of thing he wished to get involved with. Some of the druids, as the snake people called themselves, had the gift of foresight and knew their cause was lost. Because they revered many of the same things as the fae, he brought the willing back to the queen.

"Lorbeer told me of a village overrun with rats," Rosenholz said as she and Stefan sat down for breakfast.

"Rats?" Stefan asked. He hadn't had the opportunity to summon or banish rats.

Rosenholz grinned and nodded. "They're everywhere. They get in the clothes and the food, and if that weren't bad enough, they're constantly chewing and scuttling about. They nip at the children. They've killed all the cats and now they fight the dogs." She seemed delighted by the chaos. "No one can sleep through the racket."

"What is the name of this village?" Stefan asked, eager to be on his way.

"It's called Hameln," Rosenholz said. "On the river Weser."

* * *

The village of Hameln was well and truly overrun. There were easily ten times as many rats as there were people. It was a warm June day when Stefan roamed the streets, looking for the office of the burgermeister. Some folks stared at him, while others looked away. As usual, he stood out as more than a foreigner. His

56

shirt was half green and half yellow, and his trousers, shortened to the knee, were the opposite. The straps of his brown leather sandals crisscrossed up his legs. On his head, he wore a large red hat with an equally red feather. It had been a gift from Lorbeer, who had been spending a great deal of time with Rosenholz. Stefan suspected he would soon have to build his own home, and that his cousin may be less inclined to travel. That thought saddened him, but he'd learned life was full of change, and not all of it was bad. Rosenholz and Lorbeer would remain his friends, and he was ready to tend to himself.

At last, he found the town hall. He was greeted by a young woman with blue eyes and blonde hair curled in ringlets. She wore a black dress with red laces up the bodice. "I'm here about the rats," he said. "I see there are more than I thought. I assure you I have the skill to banish them."

"Do you really?" she asked, sounding both desperate and delighted. "Would you please wait here, just a moment? I'll get you in to see the burgermeister."

"Thank you."

A few minutes later the young woman returned, her face flushed and eyes bright. "Please come with me. They'll see you now."

Two men sat with the burgermeister, and all three of them looked exhausted and harried. "My daughter says you claim you can get rid of the rats," the burgermeister said, rising to his feet when Stefan stepped into the room. "Is this true? We've tried everything. Don't mistake this as a simple task. How do you intend to accomplish this?"

Stefan swept off his red hat and bowed to the men. Courtesy was simple enough, and it often made matters easier. "With naught but my pipe, I recently rid a village in Transylvania of a horde of vampire bats. My good sirs, I can certainly banish the rats of Hameln."

The burgermeister's expression turned suspicious. "Don't think you can take advantage of us in our current situation," he warned. "We'll pay nothing until you've proven your claim."

Stefan nodded. "I expected as much. However, we must

agree on the price beforehand." He took the burgermeister's shrug for acceptance. "I think one thousand marks would be sufficient payment."

"One thousand?" the burgermeister asked, his voice incredulous. "If you can rid Hameln of rats, will give you fifty thousand."

"Very well. I shall take care of the problem this very evening," Stefan said. "I must ask that the people of Hameln stay out of the streets, starting at moonrise."

"Don't want us to see what you're doing?" the burgermeister asked suspiciously.

"I welcome you to watch from your windows." Stefan smiled. "Come morning, there will be nary a rat in all of Hameln."

"Ha!" exclaimed the burgermeister. "I'd pay money to see that."

"And so you shall," Stefan replied. It occurred to him, as he walked out, that they had not even asked his name, nor where he was staying. Perhaps they assumed he would find the task too daunting and would flee in the middle of the night. Their lack of faith was disappointing, and their indifference to such basic courtesy was offensive.

Stefan spent the rest of the afternoon roaming the streets of Hameln and familiarizing himself with the lay of the village. His music needed to reach every hiding place. Hameln was large by some standards, but small compared to other places Stefan had visited. The half-timber buildings were one and two stories tall with red slate roofs. The village was quite literally next to the Weser River, which provided a perfect resolution.

He waited by the river as the day passed. Women and children came to fetch water. Parents wouldn't let their children near him, but most children were alone and freely visited him. As the day grew late, fewer came for water, and he was alone.

"May I speak with you, sir?"

Stefan turned to see the young woman from the town hall, the burgermeister's daughter. He took off his hat and swept her a formal bow.

Her pale cheeks turned pink and she took a few steps closer

to him. "I wanted to warn you," she said quietly. "My father and the others don't trust you."

"I'd noticed as much," Stefan said.

"Even if you do as you say you can, they will not be reassured," she said. "If you can get rid of the rats, they will assume you're a sorcerer and that you brought the rats to begin with."

Stefan sighed and looked out across the water. That was most unexpected. "What do you recommend?" he asked, turning back to her. He realized she was very pretty, in a way unlike the fae. "Should I not free your village of this plague? Should I leave Hameln as it is?"

Her lower lip trembled and she shook her head. "I beg you not to do that."

He realized she believed his claim, no matter what others had said. She truly feared he might leave without banishing the rats when he was fully capable of doing so. He touched her cheek, and a tear fell onto his hand. "And I beg you not to do that," he whispered.

"I can't bear to live this way any longer." She looked up into his face. "I would do anything you ask, if only you'll do what you've said you can."

Her words and the way her eyes held his, caught his breath away. He wanted to kiss her, but that would be no better than his father. He was fae and had surely charmed her to some measure, whether he meant to or not. "I have already given my word," he said quickly. "I can ask nothing more of you." He smiled, and withdrew his hand from her cheek.

"What's your name?" she asked.

"I'm Stefan."

"I'm Edelgard." She smiled and reached up to touch his chin with soft light fingers. "How is it that you have no beard? You're no boy."

"My people don't grow beards." He caught her hand, because he didn't think he could handle the pleasant distraction. He felt drawn to Edelgard, but was unsure how to proceed. He did not wish to regret his actions, and he knew too little about that which he'd carefully avoided. He only held her hand, for that did not ask or promise anything beyond the simple touch it was. When she finally left him, he couldn't keep her out of his thoughts.

Moonrise came, and Stefan walked to the end of the village farthest from the river. He lifted his golden pipe and began a song for rats. It was fast-paced and a little chaotic. He worked in repetitions for chewing and scratching, and slides from pitch to pitch for jumping. The rats squeezed under doors and scampered down the crooked narrow streets. He began a slow walk toward the river, gathering more of the plump rodents as he went. He turned to play his pipe down the side streets. People watched from their windows, entire families stood and stared in amazement as their homes were emptied. Stefan continued to play, calling still more rats from still more houses.

He paused in his walking in the center of a significant intersection. Here he allowed his music time to filter through the buildings. He chanced to look up and saw Edelgard in a second story window. Her eyes were wide as she leaned on the ledge. Stefan knew that she was not following the progression of rats. She was watching him, and he had to look away lest his music falter.

At long last, just as the stars and moon told him it was midnight, he led the rats to the bank of the Weser River. He took two steps in. Cool water rushed over his feet, still clad in sandals. Another three steps and it reached his knees. The current was strong enough to defeat the swimming skill of the charmed creatures. The rats followed him into the Weser and were washed away. Those behind could not stop despite the fate awaiting them.

When the last of the rats had been drawn underwater, Stefan finally let the last note fade. He closed his eyes and listened. Hameln was silent. He walked out of the river, letting his pipe hang against his chest from its bright strap. He had a room at an inn, and even he needed to rest after working such an extended charm. He passed under Edelgard's window and was disappointed that she wasn't there.

* * *

The next morning, Stefan returned to the town hall. Again Edelgard greeted him, and his delight in seeing her surprised him. Her smile was bright and cheerful. His heart leapt as she gladly

60

clasped his hands.

"You did it," she said, all but pulling him through the door. She didn't seem to mind when that caused him to career into her. "You said you could, you promised you would, and you did. I slept through the night for the first time in weeks." She shook her head. "And I watched you..." She ended with an exhalation, apparently at a loss for words.

Stefan wondered if she were truly so amazed by him or if he had inadvertently charmed her. He hoped it was an honest response, not one he'd forced. "I appreciate your kindness."

She showed him in to her father, once again cautioning him not to trust the man.

"I have done as promised," Stefan said. Again, the burgermeister had two others with him. "You'll find no more rats in Hameln."

"True enough," the burgermeister said.

"I'm here to collect my marks, then I must be on my way," Stefan said. He wondered about coming back to see Edelgard. Would she want him to? Was he courting trouble to think along these lines?

"Yes, well. Due to certain irregularities, we've decided to modify our original agreement," the burgermeister said, testiness creeping into his voice.

"Irregularities?" Stefan asked, alarmed.

"You didn't tell us you would be using magic," the burgermeister said.

"You didn't ask," Stefan pointed out. "And if you were concerned about the use of magic, you should have inquired in advance. How else did you think I would do it?"

"You're quite rude," the burgermeister said, rising to his feet. He was significantly shorter than Stefan and glaring up at him had less effect that he may have hoped. He quickly sat back down. "It's absurd to expect even a thousand marks for a few hours' work." He crossed his arms over his chest, glancing quickly at the others, who nodded their agreement.

"You could not have done the same in so short a time," Stefan said. "And it was no easy labor for all my speed." He'd occasionally encountered difficulties, but nothing so irritating as this. Village leaders occasionally promised payment beyond their means, and he was reasonable for all that he made certain such individuals kept their word. "We had a bargain. I fulfilled my end, and you now owe me the fifty thousand marks you offered."

"We aren't satisfied with this arrangement," the burgermeister said, his face turning red. "You may have fifty marks, or none at all."

Stefan glared at the man, lightning flashing in his eyes, and the burgermeister paled. "I shall not lighten your pockets today, I think. But make no mistake that I shall exact suitable payment." He spun and stormed out of the room, brushing swiftly past Edelgard, who had clearly been waiting for him. It would take a day or two for him to decide upon the right punishment, but the people of Hameln would learn that it was unwise to break a promise.

"Stefan, wait," Edelgard caught up with him just as he strode out of the village.

He took a deep breath, willing his anger away. Humans were always frightened of him when he lost his temper, and he didn't wish to scare her.

"My father and the others... they're greedy," she said, looking ashamed. "Since you drowned the rats, they assumed you couldn't bring them back, so it was safe to deny you your rightful payment. I heard them talking. They think it's a fabulous joke that they were able to rid the town of rats without paying for it. They think it will keep them popular with the people."

"And if the truth were out, what would the people think?" Stefan asked.

She looked at her feet. "They will agree that the burgermeister got them a bargain."

Stefan nodded. "They are free to think that for the time. I will be paid, though at this point I shall not accept money. The price of my service has gone up."

"So you'll be back?" She looked into his face, hopeful.

"On Sunday," he said. "But only for a short time."

"I'd like to see you," Edelgard said, taking his hand.

"That may not be wise." When that only caused her to smile,

he asked, "what time is the church service?"

"Eight o'clock," she replied.

"Then that's when I will return," he promised.

\* \* \*

It was precisely eight o'clock in the morning when Stefan returned to Hameln. Standing in the place he'd started his rat song, he again raised his golden pipe to his lips. This time, he played a children's song. It was cheerful and carefree, and perfect for those between the ages of four and eleven years. As he slowly walked down the street, once again in the direction of the Weser River, he gathered a following. Small feet, bare or clad in wooden shoes, skipped along behind him. Chubby little hands clapped in time with the music. Tempted by the joys of Faerie, sunshine and waterfalls, the children were bound to his will.

Edelgard stood in front of her house. Without stopping his piping, Stefan bowed to her. She looked at his entourage, then waded through the sea of children to walk beside him. As he crossed the street, Stefan noticed a little girl making slow and clumsy progress, yet still houses away. He detoured his pack of children to collect her. She had a clubfoot, and needed a crutch to walk. She moved far too slowly, but Stefan would not leave her behind. In Faerie, she could be healed. He would be unable to carry her gently while still playing his pipe, but he was willing to try. Before he could pause in his music and scoop her up, Edelgard had already done so. She settled the girl against her hip and gestured for him to continue.

At the river's edge, Stefan turned toward the north. His charges sang and danced around him, their flaxen curls bouncing on their shoulders and rosy cheeks. At long last, he had led them to the foot of Klagesberg Mountain, where a large ring of mushrooms waited. There were one hundred and thirty children in all. Never had so many been brought to Faerie at one time. He suspected the queen would be most amused with his solution. That this retribution would provide great joy in Faerie was an appreciable irony.

He herded the children into the ring, then slowed the music to put them to sleep. Edelgard still held the crippled child, now peacefully at rest. He let the tune drift off before lowering his pipe.

He looked closely at Edelgard. She had not been charmed, but had followed nonetheless. "I must leave," he said. "And I won't be back."

"Take me with you," she said. She stepped into the ring and met his eyes. "You're fae, aren't you?"

Stefan nodded. "If you come with me, you can't come back."

"I don't want to." She proudly held up her chin. Perhaps she had a charm of her own, for all she was human.

How he wanted her to come with him, but he had to be honest with her. "There are things that will be expected of you, if you return to Faerie with me," he said. He wished Rosenholz were there. He would have preferred to have her give the explanations.

"Will I become one of your many wives?" Edelgard asked, and her expression suggested that she didn't think that so bad a thing.

"We don't marry," he said, blushing. "Though you would be expected to bear children, if you can."

"Yours?" she asked.

He nodded. "They will assume that's why I brought you."

Edelgard shrugged. "I am expected to have children no matter where I am, Stefan. Hameln isn't so different from Faerie in that. But having met you, I don't wish to be with anyone else."

"You're certain?" he asked.

"Only if you wish it as well," she said.

Stefan smiled as he raised the golden pipe to his lips to play the tune that would send them all to Faerie.

# Never After: A Fairy Tale

There was once a land where magic thrived and romance was the rule. Fairy tales were historical accounts, and children patiently awaited their own happy endings.

King Nicodemus, the great grandson of Cinderella, ruled the kingdom of Amergau. In keeping with fashion of the time, his daughter Allea was betrothed to a prince of a neighboring kingdom. That taken care of, Nicodemus and his wife Cordelia prepared themselves for yet another romantic tale worthy of recording.

\* \* \*

"You looked so lovely on your betrothal day," Cordelia said as she tied her daughter's hair in rags.

Allea rolled her eyes. She'd heard the litany at least once a week at bedtime since that very day. It was as if they expected her to be delighted with the whole business. When she was little, and marriage seemed a long way off, it sounded fun. But she was eighteen now, and wasn't so sure she liked the idea of marrying someone she hadn't seen since she was six.

"Prince Torsten was so nervous he nearly dropped the ring,"

her mother giggled, as she always did, at the young prince's near mishap.

Allea's fingers went unbidden to her neck, where that same ring, now outgrown, was worn on a thin silver chain. "Mother, he was only five," she said quietly. "He was probably scared of all the people."

"The whole kingdom was there!" Cordelia crowed with delight.

She tuned out her mother as she finished getting ready for bed. After twelve years she could nod and respond appropriately without thinking. She wondered what Torsten was like now. She sincerely hoped that he'd mastered the use of silverware. Her strongest memories from that day were of the feast. He'd slopped his roast all over her dress, and he'd stepped on her toes when they danced. It hardly seemed an auspicious beginning, and of late it had become increasingly difficult to set aside reality in favor of the carefully constructed fantasy.

"Sweet dreams, dear," Cordelia said, planting a kiss on her daughter's brow. She gave the covers one final pat before putting out the bedside candle.

Allea watched her mother close and lock the iron gate that had served as her bedroom door since her betrothal. It had been her father's brilliant idea that she be "imprisoned" each night until Torsten came to "rescue" her. The metal smith had been delighted to create a special dungeon door for her room, complete with a heart motif in the grille-work. The stonemason had been equally pleased to build a mock fireplace hearth for the head of her bed.

The light from her mother's candle gradually faded down the hall. Why must they assume she had no mind of her own? What if Torsten was still a slob who couldn't dance? She had more questions about him than she could keep track of.

* * *

"What's he like?" Allea asked as she and her mother toured the garden one morning.

"Who, dear?"

"Prince Torsten. What's he like?"

Cordelia beamed at her daughter, clearly delighted with the

question. "Why I hear he's gotten quite tall," she whispered as if it were a wonderful secret.

Allea patiently waited, until she realized her mother wasn't going to add anything to that glowing accommodation. "He's tall?" she asked hesitantly.

"Umm hmm," her mother agreed with a nod. "Oh, and handsome," she added, clasping her hands together under her chin with an excess of glee.

"Tall and handsome? That's it?" She stopped and stared at her mother. "I'm supposed to marry him because he's tall and handsome? Such fine qualities; so rare and unexpected in a *prince*."

Her mother looked at her as if she'd suddenly sprouted wings. "Is something wrong, dear?"

"No, not at all," she said quickly. "Oh won't you please meet my husband Torsten. He's tall and handsome."

Cordelia eyed her daughter warily. "You're being sarcastic again, aren't you."

"Who, me?" She dramatically placed one hand on her chest. "You know I hate that."

\* \* \*

Allea waited until the light from her mother's candle had vanished and the hall was dark. No one would give her another thought until morning, and she'd be far away by then. She kicked off the covers and scrambled for the bundle of things she'd stuffed under her bed earlier. Since no one could give her satisfactory answers, she'd find out on her own. Why, not even her father had seen Torsten since the betrothal!

She hurriedly dressed in the simple clothes she'd borrowed for traveling. She'd been set up as the ideal fairy tale princess, right down to the finest details of her wardrobe. Every one of her dresses was a personally tailored patchwork of complimentary silks and satins carefully cut and frayed to give the appearance of rags. The oft repeated handkerchief hemline, varying only in number of points, emphasized this appearance. Such distinctive clothes would only make her stand out, and increased the likelihood that someone would recognize her along the way.

It wasn't the first time she'd picked the lock on her bedroom gate, although she'd been careful to keep the ability a secret. Her mother would be thrilled with that part of the retelling, she was sure. She crept through the dark halls, quickly making her way to the kitchen.

She'd bribed the stable boy to tack up her horse at dusk. He was reliable in such tasks, else she'd have spent the time to do it herself. She walked the horse slowly out of the courtyard before letting him out to a canter. The evening air was cool but refreshing, and it kept her awake as the night passed.

Shortly after dawn she reached the small inn that marked the halfway point on her map. The plump little lady behind the desk gave Allea an odd look as she approached.

"Have you any rooms?" Allea asked. She hoped a few hours rest would be sufficient. She wanted to reach Rachten before dark. She planned to stay at an inn rather than revealing herself to Torsten. Although she'd be well attended if she presented herself to the palace, she didn't want her betrothed to be forewarned and on his best behavior. She wanted to know what he was really like.

"Yes," the woman replied. "Will it be just yourself miss, or will anyone be joining you?"

"Just me," she said quickly. So the inn was that sort of place, was it? She smiled, amused. She'd best leave that part out of the tale, when relaying it to her mother. "And my horse needs a stall and a bag of oats."

The woman offered a curt nod. "And how long can we expect the honor of your visit?"

"Just a few hours." She untied the bow beneath her chin and pulled off her hat, holding it by the wide brim. "I'm afraid I've somewhere to be this evening."

"Costs the same for a night as it does for a few hours, miss. But I can send you on your way with a bit of lunch."

Allea nodded. "That will do nicely, thank you."

"And where would a nice lady such as yourself be traveling alone?" the woman asked as she pulled a brass key off its hook. "You aren't a runaway, are you?"

"Of course not," she responded, more than a little surprised. "I'm going to meet my betrothed."

"Oh, well are you then?" she asked, delighted. "How exciting at that!"

"I haven't seen him since we were children," she said, as if confiding in the woman. "And he doesn't know I'm coming," she whispered.

"Oh what a surprise you'll be to him, lass." The woman let out a gentle sigh. "That's as sweet a tale as ever I've heard." She handed Allea the key.

"What can I say," Allea asked with a sheepish smile. "I'm a romantic." She tried to keep her laughter to an appropriate shy giggle until she reached her room.

* * *

Allea had slept longer than she'd intended, but it wasn't yet noon and she had a significant head start. If her father's maps were as accurate as he always claimed, she would still make Rachten before eventide.

It also occurred to her that her parents might not have sent anyone after her, letting the course of true love prevail, and all that. She'd left a note, and she'd traveled enough in her life to be as safe as one could expect. Her mother was probably already writing letters to her friends, sharing the early details of her daughter's excursion. Father was sure to play annoyed and out-of-sorts when she returned, but she'd see the glint of mischief in his eye and know it was all for show.

The rest of the journey went smoothly. The only delay was just outside the gates of the city, where the traffic of visiting vendors and cotters forced her to slow her horse to a walk.

She thought it odd that she'd never been to Rachten in all her travels. It was closer than nearly any other city, including many towns and villages in Amergau, and she suspected her parents and Torsten's of intentionally keeping them apart. She could only guess that the mystery was supposed to build the suspense, but she questioned the tradition that would have her wed a complete stranger. She'd sent him letters, of course; had been encouraged to write him once she'd turned fourteen. In four years she'd barely received as many responses from her prospective husband. Men don't write, she was told, not the way women do. But the closer she

69

got, the more she wondered if it was a personality flaw on Torsten's part.

After acquiring directions from a street lad, she made her way to the inn closest to the palace. While she'd carefully planned the journey itself, she was undecided how to proceed now that she was in Rachten. If Torsten was the sort who rarely left the palace, she'd have no choice but to go there. After a night's rest she would be better able to decide her next step. The inn appeared to be a popular place, and she hoped she'd arrived in time to get a room.

"I've one room that can ensure you some peace, miss," the innkeeper said. He glanced nervously toward the common room where, by the sound of it, a great party was being held.

"Some is better than none, I suppose," she said as she handed him the coppers. "Is there some sort of celebration going on?" She'd expected an inn within the city to be busy, but not quite so loud.

"Not from around here, are you?" he asked with a friendly grin.

"No, I'm afraid I'm not," she admitted. "I've come to meet my betrothed."

"Here in Rachten?" he asked, his mood brightening. "Why that's wonderful. We've as lovely a public garden as you'll find in all the land," he assured her. "Be sure he takes you there for a picnic on a clear evening."

"I just hope I'll recognize him when I do find him."

"Don't you know what he looks like?" he asked in delighted surprise. "Why that's absolutely charming... but, however will you find him? Do you, by chance, have a glass slipper?"

She shook her head with a smile. "I'm afraid not. But I've been told that he's tall and handsome, and that the rest is irrelevant," she said with a laugh. "I'm sure I'll manage."

"I do hope so," he said fervently as he handed her the key. "Oh, you should have this," he said as he held out a red silk rosebud. "All the betrothed ladies of Rachten wear them."

She smiled as she took the flower. "Why thank you ever so much. I'm sure this will bring me all the luck I require."

"Do let me know if there's anything else you need. I'd be

honored to help you with your search."

When she stabled her horse, she noticed that nearly all the stalls were full, and the occupants were clearly of noble stock. She wondered if their owners were causing the commotion in the inn.

By the time she got cleaned up for dinner, the inn's celebrants had become even more raucous. She shrugged, resigning herself to the racket in the common room. At a cluster of small tables sat a group of young men and women, very near her in age. They wore fine linen and lace, indicative of wealth and status. They were the source of the noise, and from the number of bottles on the tables, she expected they would only get louder and more obnoxious as the night wore on. There were three ladies and five gentlemen in all, and she was astonished to see the women eschewing chairs to sit on their escorts' laps, especially in a public place. For her mother's sake, she'd leave that bit of the story out as well.

Although she was accustomed to her presence being noticed, she didn't care for the sudden silence as she crossed the room. She walked to the table farthest from the group, and attempted to ignore them as she sat down and picked up the listing of the evening's fare. In a few minutes the clamor had resumed.

She'd made it through dinner and was starting on a piece of pie when she realized one of the cads was approaching her table. She glanced up, groaning inwardly at his slow and clumsy progress. He was drunk, and he was on his way to visit her. She looked away, hoping he would change his mind.

He pulled an empty chair over to her small table, sloppily dragging it across the wooden floor. He dropped himself into the chair, letting out a little grunt as he did so.

She glared at him, thoroughly disgusted. His light brown hair had been neatly trimmed, but was darkly wet around his face. She wasn't sure if it was sweat or wine, and she didn't care to find out. He might have been handsome if his face weren't so flushed and his expression something other than drunken idiocy. "It is usually customary to request permission before joining a lady at her table," she said sternly.

He smiled and ignored her reprimand. "What I can't figure out is why a pretty little lady like you would be eating dinner all alone."

"I choose to eat alone."

"I saw you come in. You travel alone, as well. Brave girl," he said appreciatively. His ability to speak appeared unaffected by his drinking, unlike more useful faculties such as tact and coordination. Although she considered the possibility that he didn't have those to begin with. He reached across the table for her hand, knocking over the pepper grinder in the process. "Tell me something, doll-face. Do you sleep alone, too?"

Allea yanked her hand free and stood up in one swift movement. She snatched her glass off the table and splashed the wine in his face. While he dealt with the sting of wine in his eyes, she stalked out of the dining room.

She was filing her complaint with the innkeeper when the drunk caught up with her.

"C'mon, doll-face," he said with a smile. "I just wanted to let you know you could count on me for anything you might *need*."

"Leave her be," the innkeeper snapped.

The man looked at the innkeeper as if just noticing him. "I'm only having some fun, Robert," he insisted as if the innkeeper were a complete spoilsport. With a swiftness that belied his state of inebriation, he closed the distance between himself and Allea. "I want you to have fun too, pretty little doll-face. And I can make sure you do."

He pulled her roughly to him, and the nearly visible alcohol fumes on his breath made her eyes water. She pushed against his chest, but he didn't seem to notice.

"What do you say, we go up to your room for a while," he suggested as one hand fumbled with the clip in her hair. He kissed her then.

Outraged, Allea bit him. He jerked his face away in shock, but she was through being polite. She brought her knee up between his legs as hard as she could, just the way her father had explained. He fell to the floor, gasping for air.

"Faugh!" She stuck out her tongue and spat at him a couple of times, trying to clear the taste from her mouth. "I wouldn't bed you if you were my own husband!"

"Are you all right miss?" the innkeeper asked, horrified. He quickly stepped between her and the man on the floor, giving the drunk a quick glance.

"I'm fine," she said, trying not to gag on her revulsion. "Or I will be as soon as I get rid of this taste." From the tang on his lips, he must have been eating pipe burnings along with his liquor.

"Oh here," the innkeeper reached over the counter and grabbed some peppermint sticks from the jar. "I'm so sorry."

"You can't be accountable for all your guests." She scowled at the drunk who was finally trying to get up. "You try kissing me again and I'll stab you."

He only grunted in response.

"Don't think I won't," she warned as she turned purposefully toward the stairs.

"I've had it with you, prince," the innkeeper said firmly. "I'll not have my good honest business ruined on your account."

Allea paused at the bottom of the stairs. The drunk man was a prince, and a local from the sounds of it. She knew Rachten had at least two princes, and she was not betrothed to the oldest of them. How many brothers did Torsten have?

"It's bad enough you come in here with *those* girls and make all that noise. You've given my inn a bad name, and I never agreed to that." He hauled the prince to his feet. "Your parents persuaded me to let you have your little parties here, but that was with the understanding you'd leave the rest of my guests alone."

"C'mon Robert, I didn't hurt anyone," he insisted, still half hunched over.

"You can spend the night, cause lord knows I won't be held responsible if you break your neck falling off that horse of yours. But that's it. You can't come back."

"But Robert " he protested, sounding like a spoiled child.

"No, Prince Torsten. Like every other innkeeper in Rachten, I've had it with you. Your parents will just have to endure your little romps themselves from now on. They never should have pushed that responsibility on to us good honest citizens." He turned back to Allea. "You sure you're okay miss? You look awful pale."

She nodded absently. This drunken graceless slob was

Prince Torsten? "I... I'm going to retire now." She turned and managed not to trip on her way up the stairs. She could hear Torsten and the innkeeper arguing yet, but she wasn't listening. She locked her door and sat on the bed. She was betrothed to a wine slurping pig-dog who regularly hung around with women of questionable behavior. He'd made a pass at her. And she'd bit him.

She started to giggle, which eventually turned to weeping. Whether it was the irony of her first meeting with her prospective husband or distress, she cried herself to sleep for the first time in her life.

* * *

Although convinced that Torsten had no redeeming qualities, she felt obligated to investigate further before returning to Amergau. She didn't know what she would do if he really was as bad as he'd appeared last night. *How* would she tell her parents?

Most of Torsten's entourage was in the common room when she walked in, although he was absent. Allea assumed he was either sleeping off his indulgence, or dead of alcohol poisoning. As a group they looked sullen, and she suspected they were all nursing headaches.

In walking past their table she tripped over a nearby chair, which fell to the floor with a bang. She giggled, as if embarrassed and settled herself at the next table over. While waiting for her breakfast, she rearranged her place setting a number of times, clattering the cup and saucer together and clanking the silverware. After several minutes of silence, she knocked her plate off the table, and she couldn't quite hide her grin when the crash made Torsten's friends jump.

After a quick meal, she went down to the stable to check on her horse. She opened the door and found herself facing Torsten. She took a step back and eyed him warily. He'd evidently fared better than his friends, although that likely meant he was more accustomed to drunken carousing.

Her mother had been right. He was tall. Likewise, he could have been handsome without half trying. "Looking for someone?" he asked quietly. His smile might have been nice, if it weren't so condescending

"Most certainly not," she replied as if insulted.  "I came to check on my horse."

He shrugged but stepped to the side to let her through.

She wasn't altogether sure she wanted to be alone in the stable with him, but she refused to fear him.  She walked by him to the stall where her horse was happily munching on a bag of oats.  She checked his water supply and nodded, satisfied.

"If horses are what you like, why didn't you say so," Torsten asked, as he leaned on the wall opposite her.  "Some have likened me to a horse."

"In intelligence?" she asked.

"No."  He stretched, putting his hands behind his head.  "In physical attributes."

She stared at him.  *This* was what she was supposed to marry?  "Prince Torsten," she began.

"You know who I am," he sounded pleased.  He pushed himself away from the wall.  "As a prince I have a better chance with you then?  I can promise you a great many things, but," he cautioned, holding up a finger, "only if you're careful not to call out anyone else's name but mine."

"Prince Torsten," she snapped.  "My horse is a gelding," she said firmly.  "I haven't the patience for a stallion."

He stopped, staring at her in surprise.

"You're mistaken if you think I would swoon for the likes of you," she said with as much contempt as she could muster.  "Even if I were inclined, which I certainly am not, I'm betrothed."  She pointed to the rosebud she'd pinned to her dress that morning.

He shrugged.  "Everyone in this land is betrothed.  Even me."

"Yet you betray her?"

He shrugged again.  "It's an arranged marriage.  There's no love between us.  We haven't even seen each other since we were kids."

"Then why haven't you released her from that contract?" she demanded.

He let out a laugh, as if she'd made a terrific joke.  "When I marry Allea, I'll get my own kingdom and more power than I ever could have expected here. Of course I'm going to marry her," he said scornfully. "She'll be my wife and she'll give me a couple of kids, but that's all." He took a step closer to her. "What I do with my time, is my business."

When he kissed her this time, she grabbed the dagger at his belt and stuck it in his thigh. He yowled like a wounded animal and fell to the ground, both hands clutching at his leg.

"What did you do that for?" he demanded. "I wasn't hurting you!"

"I warned you last night," she snapped. She hurriedly tacked up her horse.

"You can't expect me to remember everything from last night!"

She looked at him. "Oh. The poor princeling has amnesia?" She tucked the bit in her horse's mouth. "Guess you shouldn't have had so much to drink, now, should you?"

"Aw, c'mon," he begged. "It was a party."

"You party entirely too often, Prince Torsten." She walked her horse out of the stable, then returned to his side for a moment. "I need a souvenir, you know," she said with a smile just before she pulled the dagger out of his leg. He let out another cry, but his complaints fell on deaf ears. She rolled the knife up in a handkerchief, then waved cheerfully to him on her way out of the stable.

"You can't leave me here like this!"

"Don't bet on it."

"But I'm to be a king!" he roared.

She gathered her belongings and checked out of the inn.

\* \* \*

It was dark and she hadn't seen another traveler in hours. At first she'd been so angry she could hardly stand it, and she fled from Rachten out of fear of what she might do. She'd actually stabbed another person, and her betrothed at that. Now that her adventure was beginning to sink in, she was nearly overwhelmed with self-pity and uncertainty. How could he not love her? How could he be so dreadful? And how under the stars was she going to tell her parents? She was trembling when she tugged on her horse's reins to stop for a rest.

She slid from the saddle, nearly stumbling, and the jolt forced out a sob that seemed to have been stuck in her throat for some time. It led the way for many others, and she stood in the road, clinging to her reins, crying.

A pale blue light slowly grew around her, calling her attention back to the present, and she struggled to control herself. She glanced up to see an old woman with a small lantern approaching from the woods. Only magic could explain such a small device casting so great a light, and in such a color, she ducked her head behind her horse's and hastily wiped the tears from her cheeks.

Not about to be eluded, the woman stepped around the horse. "Poor dear," the woman muttered. "Come, come. It does no good to hide from me," she said with a gentle voice.

Allea sniffled and looked up. "Who are you?"

The woman offered her a kindly smile. "Why I'm your fairy godmother, of course." She reached out and took Allea's hand.

"I have a fairy godmother?" She was genuinely surprised.

Still smiling, the woman nodded. "Oh yes. I've been in the family for centuries."

"Oh!"

"Now there's no sense in beating around the bush with me Allea. I know you're upset." She looked disgusted. "Back in the old days, that young rake wouldn't have kept his title what with his carrying on. And his parents never would have let you be deceived so." She sighed and shook her head sadly. "But times have changed."

"Can you help me?" Allea asked, desperate for any source of hope.

Her godmother smiled placidly. "That's why I'm here, my dear. And you might say that good magic is my speciality."

"What do I need to do?" Allea asked. "Have you a spell that will mend all this? I'd kiss a frog... although kissing a prince didn't seem to help. Wishing on a star? Salt over my shoulder? Pennies in a fountain? I have lots of pennies..."

"Oh no, nothing like that."

"What then?"

"You have to look inside yourself for the magic, dear."

She stared at her godmother for a moment. "What?"

"You're much stronger than you realize. It's time you freed yourself from all these unfair expectations."

"Free myself?" she asked, suddenly feeling quite alone. "Aren't you going to help me? Isn't that your job?"

"It's my job to make you happy, my dear, and there's no way for you to be happy with Torsten. I don't think any woman could be."

Allea sighed. "I guess he is pretty much beyond hope."

"I don't guess, dear, I know. And so should you. You need to trust yourself more." She reached into one sleeve and pulled out a thin blue wand. "Now, I can't find the magic for you, only you can do that. But I can get you off on the right foot." She tapped the silver chain around Allea's neck, and it fell to the ground.

It felt odd not to have the necklace on, and she gently rubbed her neck.

Her godmother picked up the chain and ring and held it out to her. "That's what freedom feels like, dear. A little strange at first, but you'll grow to like it; it's worth fighting for. Remember that."

* * *

It was mid afternoon when Allea returned home. She was tired of the whole business, and it wasn't over yet. She found her parents in the garden, enjoying their tea.

"Allea!" her mother stood up and reached for her hands. "Dear one, I've been so worried!"

"Thank the fairies that you're home safely," her father whispered as he embraced her.

She sat down at the table with a sigh. Her backside hurt from the riding and her legs had gone wobbly. She still wasn't sure how she was going to explain the whole mess.

After several minutes, her mother broke the silence. "And what did you think of Prince Torsten?"

She looked at each of her parents in turn, then looked down at the gray flagstones beneath her feet. She took a deep breath, gathering her courage. She wished she could believe that she was as strong as her fairy godmother claimed she was. "I won't marry him."

"What happened?" her father asked quickly.

She looked up again. "He made a pass at me. And I bit him."

Her father coughed, hastily covering his mouth with a napkin. "You bit him?"

"Maybe he was so overjoyed by your presence that his exuberance merely *seemed* inappropriate," Cordelia suggested.

"No. That's not it at all." Allea stood up, straightening her stiff legs. "He didn't even know who I was. He just wants to be a king."

"You're sure?" Nicodemus asked. "Maybe you just caught him on a bad day."

Allea let out a disgusted sigh. "If I marry him I'll spend the rest of my life saying things like, my husband drinks a wee bit too much." For once her sarcasm wasn't delivered with a smile. "Though that's not quite right." She stood for a moment, thinking. She had to make them understand. "Hello, I'm Prince Torsten's baby-maker. I'm afraid he's off spending my money on wine and other women," she said with false brightness. Then she looked at each of them. "Is that what you want?"

Her parents shook their heads simultaneously, too stunned to speak.

"I won't be treated like that," she said firmly. "I deserve better."

"Dear, are you sure you're all right?" her father asked slowly.

"No. I'm not sure." She'd done a lot of thinking after meeting her fairy godmother, but she still felt confused and disoriented. Her whole world had changed so quickly, and she didn't know how to respond to it. "But I won't marry him. You'll have to write his parents and let them know. He's free to find another contract, if anyone will have him."

\* \* \*

When Prince Torsten came to Amergau to plead his case, Allea wouldn't even see him. She gave her father two things to present to her former betrothed as her response to his request that she reconsider her decision. The first was a broken silver chain with a small ring. The second item was a wooden box. Inside was Torsten's dagger, still wrapped in her handkerchief.

When he realized what had happened, his enraged curse echoed all the way to Allea's drawing room upstairs. That one word seemed to break ground for a string of swearing that accompanied him out, and Allea was sure she heard him cursing still, as he rode down the road.

After Torsten had been dismissed, Nicodemus sent out letters announcing a feast in honor of summer. He casually mentioned that his daughter was no longer engaged, and that suitors might wish to present themselves at the festival.

Allea was livid once she found out. "Don't I have any say in this?" she demanded, brandishing the invitation she'd found, as if it were a weapon.

"It's up to you this time," her father answered. "I've only invited them here so you can meet them."

"We're just asking you to give them a chance," her mother said quickly. "It can't hurt to be nice to them and see who they are. We're not expecting you to make any rush decisions." She glanced at her husband. "And you may as well look, or you'll never find your true love."

She scowled at her mother. "I don't know that I believe in true love anymore."

"How can you say that?" asked her mother in shock. "Why your great-great..."

"My great-great grandmother was a ditz who couldn't keep her shoes on her feet."

"Grandmother Cinderella was a good woman," Nicodemus reprimanded her. "And she found true love when she least expected to."

"Fine," she reluctantly agreed. "I'll be nice. But I won't guarantee that I'll fall in love."

\* \* \*

Her mother's assurances not to get pushy lasted approximately two days.

"Prince Felipo is a handsome one, isn't he?" Cordelia asked

her daughter over lunch. She smiled eagerly. "He'd make a good match."

"All Prince Felipo cares about is jousting and wrestling," she said in disgust. "Jousting this, and jousting that. And his cousin Akilah is scarcely any better."

"That's *Prince* Akilah," her mother corrected absently.

"I don't know when I've seen him that his head wasn't full of mead. He could drown half the kingdom in what he drinks in a day."

"He doesn't drink that much," Cordelia insisted.

"Torsten drank less than Akilah," she countered.

"Well, what about Duke Kechu?" her mother asked. "He doesn't seem all that interested in sports, and I've never seen him drink in excess."

"He's sweet on prince William." She nearly laughed at her mother's horrified expression. "What? Watch him and you'll see. He prefers the company of his own."

Cordelia covered her discomfort with a cough. "Duke Gunnar's a nice young man."

"He's the fool in the fable, and he's probably as much after my money as anything else."

"Allea, he's a duke. He has money."

"What he's got is debt. Puts far too much on the horses, and the odd card game, and the occasional fencing match, even children practicing marksmanship." She grinned. "He lost a five-piece to me this very morning."

"Duke Mukunza?" her mother asked, clearly desperate.

"Have you seen that man's temper?" Allea asked, appalled. "He'll beat anything within reach when he's gone sour. Why I bet he'd kill me if I gave him a daughter instead of a son."

"Well there must be someone suitable," Cordelia insisted.

"Not in that lot." She rolled her eyes and shrugged. "Besides, who says I have to be married to be happy?"

Cordelia stared at her daughter, visibly distraught. "That's the way things work. They always have."

"Maybe they don't have to work that way."

\* \* \*

It had been three weeks since the summer festival debacle, when Allea finally approached her parents in their throne room. "I've reached a decision," she announced. "I'm not getting married," she paused at her mother's horrified gasp. "Not unless I find someone I'm sure about."

"But you have to marry," her father said, rising out of his seat. "Crown princesses must marry."

"Why?" she demanded. She'd known they wouldn't like it, and she might have to fight to get her way. She'd actually made up her mind weeks ago, but it had taken until now for her to gather the strength to face her parents.

"It's just the way things are done," he said.

Allea drew herself up to her full height and met her father's eyes. Since breaking off her engagement with Torsten, she'd abandoned a lot of the conventions that had been thrust upon her. She finally felt like her own person, and her fairy godmother was right. Freedom was worth fighting for. "You can't make me."

"We have been lenient with you, Allea," her father began, clearly furious. "Perhaps too lenient. But you *will* wed. If I have to choose your husband, so be it, but you will take him."

"If that's the way you truly feel, then I'm leaving." Allea crossed her arms over her chest. It was no mere gamble. She was now ready to throw away her birthright if necessary. "I don't need to be a crown princess and I don't want a husband. Without me, you'll have to deal with the chaos of finding a new heir, and I'm sure the cousins will be along shortly to make things difficult for you." She knew she'd won when her father paled and sat down with a sigh.

Cordelia caught her daughter's arm. "Don't do this."

"It's no longer my choice," Allea said. "It's up to you. If you agree to this, I'll stay."

"But you'll be unhappy." The concern was clear on her mother's face.

Allea smiled. "No." She nearly laughed at her parents' astonishment. "Don't you realize, I don't need to be married to be happy. I've always been happy doing the things I like to do."

"But you had Torsten to look forward to," her father suggested, sounding reasonable.

"He was never real to me." She shrugged. "And making him real didn't exactly help."

"But you'll be lonely," her mother suggested.

"I have my friends. I have you." She shook her head and smiled. "I'm happy just like this. Right now. There's no need to change it."

\* \* \*

Princess Allea, who needed no knight to rescue her, never married. She lived happily ever after, demonstrating that a damsel needn't find a prince to obtain happiness.

## The End

## *What Large Teeth*

There was once a great wolf who lived in a lush green forest. He was much like other wolves, embracing the freedom of night runs and enjoying routine meals of hare and the occasional deer. As a youth, he had left his pack to find his fortune in the wide world. Many of the woodland villages boasted the position of a town wolf, but time and again he was turned down. He was told he lacked the necessary qualifications or skill set, his personality wouldn't mesh with the other staff, or in the few honest cases, he was just too damn big. Disillusioned, he settled under the canopy of green where he didn't have to interact with many humans.

His nearest neighbor was an old woman who insisted that everyone simply call her Grandma. She was a witch, rapidly approaching retirement, and feared nothing and no one. To her credit, she was able to see past the fur, canine teeth, and impressive stature to appreciate the wolf as another of the forest's valuable inhabitants. She welcomed her wild neighbors, both near and far, for polite conversation, meals, and the exchange of favors. Wolf had made a habit of fetching supplies from greater distances to save her arthritic joints the long journey. In return, she provided routine medical treatment and advice.

Grandma's granddaughter dwelt in a nearby town with her parents and three younger siblings, though she often traveled the forest path. The ability to learn and perform magic skipped every other generation, making the granddaughter the next witch in the family. Her training under Grandma had been progressing along the usual lines, though Grandma expressed concern over what she had perceived as a cruel nature housed within a charming and adorable countenance.

On her walks to Grandma's house, the granddaughter was known to magically bind small creatures unfortunate enough to come into her view. Although she released them upon her arrival for her lessons, she delighted in forcing the animals to do her will, particularly when it contrasted with the creature's own nature. Grandma confronted her granddaughter after receiving a reluctant yet adamant group complaint, but the girl feigned an innocence which Grandma didn't believe for an instant.

In that day, witches proudly wore bright red cloaks to indicate their station. In addition to being a cheery becoming color, it was an effective advertising campaign. Traveling witches, or those new to town, could be easily identified by those seeking their services. In an effort to alert the inhabitants of the forest, Grandma granted her granddaughter her novice witch's cloak when she was still quite young. This allowed her to be seen from a distance through the undergrowth, and the woodland dwellers had been warned to avoid her.

The villagers, who doted upon the lovely granddaughter, with her golden ringlets, fair face, and bright blue eyes, took to calling her Little Red Riding Hood. At the age of seventeen, she was everyone's darling. Men and boys desired her while girls and women wished to be like her. Grandma's efforts to temper Little Red's mean streak met with mixed success. Her nasty tricks grew less frequent but they took on a more vicious flavor and were more carefully concealed.

"I must ask you a favor, Wolf, my dear," Grandma said one morning as she took delivery of several bunches of fresh herbs. "And it's not something easy, this time."

Keeping all four feet on the floor, as was polite, Wolf leaned across the table so he could smell her better. He stopped short of touching her with his blunt black nose. "What is it?"

She looked down at her fingers, separating stems, before raising her head to look at him. "I'm expecting my granddaughter today." She folded her fingers together and sat down in her usual chair. "She's up to something. I've sensed it during her last several visits, and I fear that whatever it is, it can't possibly be good."

Wolf shifted his weight back and sat down. "What do you want me to do?"

"Would you be willing to accompany her along the path to my cottage?" Grandma asked. She didn't look away, but the concern over her request was evident on her lined round face. The lips, normally spread into a wide smile, were pressed together in a small wrinkled oval. She had the same blue eyes as her granddaughter, but they held a depth Little Red's lacked.

"Do you want me to follow from a distance, and watch?" Wolf asked, guessing there was more to it than that. "Or do you wish for a genuine escort?" He didn't relish the thought of getting any closer to Little Red than he had to.

She frowned, then reluctantly said, "I think it would be best if she knows you're there."

Wolf studied his front left paw, his eyes half lidded. He didn't want to appear to be a coward, but there were some things it was sensible to be frightened of, and that young woman was one of them. "I don't wish to fall under her spell," he said, after careful consideration.

"Her charms have only worked on small creatures," Grandma said. "No one larger than a badger has been controlled by her whims." She smiled, a pleased, yet conflicted expression. "She lacks the focus to bind the greater beasts of the forest, something I have not felt it necessary or wise to point out to her." She took a deep breath, letting it out slowly. "But I would be lying if I said you were perfectly safe with that granddaughter of mine. I suspect she has hidden some of her skills, quite probably gleaned from ill-advised sources."

Wolf stood up and paced through the kitchen, then back

again. He did not like this request.

"I just want you to keep an eye on her. You are an impressive sight, my dear, and I think even she would think twice before trying something unsavory under your nose." Grandma stood up, brushing her hands off on the white apron that covered her blue skirt. "Perhaps if you told her I sent you to protect her from the bears, or something. You know how those villagers are terrified of things in the forest. They filled their wolf post with a runt, as you know. There are dogs bigger than their wolf." She shook her head, and her pure white ringlets bounced in response. "You should be able to pick anything you like."

Wolf ceased his pacing, stopping to stand directly in front of Grandma. Like many witches, she was petite. Unlike most women who attained her age, she wasn't frail or curved in the spine. If he dropped his shoulders as though stalking, he could look her in the eye, which he did now. "I'll be honest," he said. "I don't like this. But I'll do it for you. You've been a good friend, and I'm willing to help if I can."

Grandma reached out and brushed the back of her index finger against the side of his muzzle, downward in the direction the hair grew. "Thank you." She opened one of the small drawers in the enormous spice cabinet that covered one whole wall of her kitchen. "I will not send you entirely unprotected, just in case," she said. "Stick out your tongue."

She dropped a pinch of crushed dried leaves on his tongue. It was bitter, and he licked at his teeth for a few moments to get rid of the taste. Then he went out to wait along the path, not far from the village.

The morning was waning when Little Red finally put in an appearance. Wolf had watched her many times from a distance. When she was still quite small, she routinely skipped the whole way whilst humming chipper little tunes that seemed so sweet and innocent, yet somehow filled him with revulsion and dread. She'd gone through a phase where she took tiny sideways steps on the balls of her feet, occasionally spinning, in a twisted sort of dance to Grandma's house. That had been followed by attempts to appear as though she were floating, gliding effortlessly down the path. That had been her least successful experiment, and she'd quickly given it up for a more purposeful stride. It had clearly become her preferred method.

Today she carried a medium-sized basket in her left hand. Its contents were concealed beneath a white towel. In her right hand she carried a bouquet of wildflowers. Her red cloak was tied at her neck, the hood hanging between her shoulders to lay her blonde curls bare.

While she was still some distance away, Wolf strode out to stand in the path. He sat and patiently waited. He was pleased to see that she looked startled, if only for a moment. "Good morning, Miss Riding Hood," he said, inclining his head in greeting.

"And good morning to you, Mr. Wolf." She flashed him a smile, dazzling yet cold. "What brings you out at this time? I thought your kind preferred the darker hours."

It took an effort to hold back the smile, an expression most humans did not understand. "I enjoy many hours of the day and night. The variety keeps me young." He lifted himself to all four feet as she approached, just in case he needed to spring away. "But I'm here specifically at your grandmother's request."

Little Red stopped. She tilted her head to the side, just a bit, while looking at him as though trying to read his mind. It was one of the expressions the townsfolk found so charming. "Why would Grandma send you?"

He had chosen his excuse in advance, one recommended by Grandma herself, and which would not place blame or danger on any of the area's current residents. "An enormous bear has been seen in this part of the wood. He is easily twice my size. Have you not heard?" he asked, feigning surprise. He had yet to run into bears as large as he described and suspected the giant Ursa had emigrated to the north long before his own kin made that journey. "The woodsman hunts him even now, for he is a fiercely dangerous beast."

"Really?" Little Red asked, her eyes wide with excitement. "You must tell me more."

"Do you know of the woodsman's sister? She lives deeper in the forest than Grandma." He waited for the young woman's eager nod to continue. "The bear happened upon her children, a twin boy and girl, only yesterday." He shook his head, as though unable to go on.

"What happened?"

"The bear ate them up," Wolf said simply. It was the most absurd thing he could think of, though he suspected a human might find it quite reasonable.

"Truly?" Little Red asked, too awed to fully hide her delight over such an event.

"There wasn't so much as a scrap left when he was through," Wolf added, thinking it would add to the horror.

"How dreadful," she murmured, her expression turning calculating.

After a moment of silence he looked down the path toward Grandma's house. "Come, we mustn't dally. Grandma is waiting, and she will worry if we are overlong in arriving." They walked together, side by side down the path, making good time. "My what a fine cloak you wear, Miss Riding Hood," Wolf said, trying to make polite conversation.

"All the better to show off my rank," she replied, beaming with delight and holding out her arms to allow for a lovely draping effect. "My mother had it sewn for my birthday. My old one was quite worn and far too simple. This is the finest brocade to be found. It suits me, don't you think?"

Wolf nodded in agreement. "What lovely flowers you have," he said, though some were brown tinged and losing their petals.

"The better to cheer Grandma," Little Red replied, admiring them for a few paces. "She seems so glum at times, cooped up out here in the forest."

"And what a large basket you have," he said. The contents smelled delicious, and he wondered if she were bringing treats or if it were simply her own lunch.

"All the better to bring biscuits to Grandma," she said. "I made them this morning, so they'd be fresh."

"They do smell fresh," he agreed. Perhaps he should ask Grandma to make him biscuits for dinner. They weren't the sort of thing a wolf should eat every day, surely, but he wasn't averse to expanding his palate.

"Would you like one?" Little Red asked, untucking the end of the towel with one finger.

"I couldn't," Wolf said. "But thank you."

"But you must have one," she said. "You've come all this way to protect me."

He didn't trust her food, no matter how good it smelled. "I couldn't eat Grandma's biscuits. It wouldn't seem right." That was a good excuse.

Little Red bit her lip for moment as though she were thinking. "You know, I'm not even sure if they turned out very well. I'd hate to give them to Grandma if they're awful. Won't you try just one, so you can tell me how they are?"

She was crafty. But he was, after all, a wolf and did not lack for craft of his own. "I shall eat one if you eat one," he suggested. "After all, my sense of taste is very different from yours. I'd hate to tell you that they're fabulous only to find that they aren't what biscuits should taste like at all."

After another moment of thought, Little Red nodded. "Very well." Nestled among the biscuits was a little pot of butter. She dipped two biscuits into the butter, then handed one to Wolf.

He held it on the top of his paw, looked it over and sniffed it thoroughly. She was already eating hers, so he devoured his in one bite. He licked his lips. "Wonderful," he assured her. "Grandma will be pleased."

"Do you really think so?" she asked. "Would you like another?"

"I couldn't," he said.

"Oh, but you must," she insisted. "You've been so kind."

"Only if you have one as well," he replied. So they each had another biscuit, and another. The supply was quite depleted when Wolf suggested they needed to hurry along. "We'd best save the last few for Grandma." His suggestion seemed to disappoint Little Red, though she didn't say so.

They walked quickly and soon they had arrived at Grandma's cottage. As they neared the door, Wolf was suddenly very tired. It was with great effort that he lifted each foot for the last few steps.

He felt hot, as he never had before. It wasn't the heat of a warm summer's day or the exertion of a long run. He could feel the blood coursing through his body, leaving a burning a trail in its wake. His stomach was heavy, as if he'd swallowed stones instead of biscuits. He turned to look at Little Red, and his vision swam, images swirling before him. When things became clear again, he could see the she looked distracted, and her cheeks were flushed.

"And how do you feel, my wolf?" she asked, her voice slow and drawling.

In that moment, he realized how monstrous a creature she was. She'd been willing to take her own poison, or potion, to trick him. It didn't matter whether she simply wanted to see what she could do, or if she had some darker purpose for him, it was all the same in his mind. He felt the hair on the back of his neck stand up, tugging at his skin and making it prickle. His lips curled back to display his curved canine teeth, larger than her biggest fingers. But when he would have lunged at her, torn out her throat, he found himself unable to move.

A strange sound hurt his ears, and he realized Little Red was laughing. Those who had been taken in by her trickery might have thought it a gay happy noise, but to him it was only evil.

"Are you angry?" she asked in a sultry whisper. "Are you vicious?"

A low growl rolled from his throat. If he could only take a step toward her, that was all he needed to close the distance. But his paws were not his own.

"Very well then," Little Red said. "I believe you're ready to pay a visit to Grandma. You may not be a giant bear, but you'll do quite nicely. And no one will suspect me." She caressed his face.

He tried to snap at her, but failed.

Little Red turned the knob and pushed the door open. "Grandma, I'm here," she called.

Wolf let out a howl, and wasn't sure who was more surprised, himself or Little Red. Perhaps her control was not so perfect, for all that she had succeeded in enraging him. Before he had a chance to give it much thought, he was bounding into the cottage, his tormentor following.

"Wolf, what's wrong?" Grandma asked, backing away as she read his body language.

He rolled his eyes as he stalked her around the table, growling without meaning to.

"What have you done?" Grandma demanded, looking at Little Red. "Release him!"

Little Red laughed. "And have him kill me? I don't think so."

"This is no way for proper witch to behave," Grandma chastised. "What do you hope to prove?"

"I don't wish to prove anything," Little Red replied. "You have nothing more to teach me. You can't even protect yourself from me. I don't need you anymore."

"If that's how you feel, I invite you to go off on your own." Grandma continued to circle the table, slowly followed by Wolf who was followed by Little Red. "Go, seek your fortune. See how far this kind of behavior gets you."

"Why should I seek my own fortune when I can have yours?" Little Red asked. "You've lived for far too long. Every year my inheritance dwindles. That doesn't suit me at all."

Wolf was getting angrier by the moment, but he wasn't entirely lost to the rage. He found he had some control over his actions, particularly when they were only a slight variation off what Little Red intended. She tried to make him grab at Grandma's ankle with his teeth, but he was able to redirect himself at the last moment to grab the leg of the chair. It wasn't great power, but it was a start.

"This sort of greed and control will get you nowhere worth going," Grandma said.

Little Red's laughter grated in Wolf's ears and made his toenails ache. He would have flinched, had he been able to. He was so hot now, he could barely see straight. His breath made his throat and mouth sting.

"Why would I wish to settle down and make do as a country witch?" Little Red demanded.

"It's made me quite comfortable," Grandma said.

Little Red scowled. "I'm meant for better. The sale of your estate, such as it is, should allow me to travel in style. There's a whole world I haven't explored yet."

Grandma nodded in agreement. "And folks you haven't exploited."

"It's my life!" Little Red snapped, her temper apparently getting better of her. "And it's my power to do with as I please."

The part of Wolf's mind that could still function, wondered if she was being mastered by the same rage she'd inflicted upon him. Perhaps it would upset her focus just enough for him to break free. But the heat and anger made it difficult for him to concentrate, much less remember from moment to moment that he needed some sort of plan. He abruptly leapt to the top of the table, something he never would have dreamed of doing himself. His ears nearly brushed the rafters. He felt his hind legs bunching to lunge, and knew Little Red was done playing with them.

He was going to have to eat Grandma, there was no doubt about that, but he thought he might have a choice in how it was done. He briefly considered attempting to make it as swift and painless as possible, but at the last moment decided to swallow her whole in the hope that she might survive.

Wolf gagged and writhed as Grandma went down his throat. He thought his heart might burst with the pain, which lasted well after he'd swallowed her down. Horrified by what he'd been made to do, he fell back on the instinct of a trapped and wounded animal. He caught the scent of Little Red behind him. She was sweaty and acrid, a repulsive combination that came from mixing magic and hate. He spun toward her, hackles raised, and a growl of his own rolled past his teeth. He took a slow steady step toward her, then another. Her slightly vacant expression turned to one of concentration, then panic.

"Back, Wolf!" she ordered, holding up her hands.

But he had read her body language and knew she no longer had control. It had taken everything she had to command him in his rage for the little time that she had done so. If she'd been quick, she might have been able to get him out of the cottage before her strength broke, but now it was too late. He sprung upon her, swallowing her even more quickly than Grandma. Again, his throat stretched and hurt as though he were eating giant porcupines whole.

Although it was justifiable, the part of his mind that was still sane was sickened and disgusted with himself as well as Little Red. He let out a howl of infinite anguish before collapsing to the floor in a fit of seizures. He thrashed like some enormous furred trout left on the shore, knocking over furniture and breaking things, all the while letting out a piteous cry. The rage had left him, and he lay spent and twitching on the floor when he smelled the arrival of the woodsman.

For a moment, it appeared as though the woodsman was simply going to chop off his head, and Wolf lay, helpless to stop him. His tongue lolled sideways out of his mouth and he could not speak to explain away the damning evidence. But the man stayed his killing blow, setting aside his axe in favor of a long sharp knife. With a careful hand, he sliced open Wolf's belly. It hurt terribly, but again he was unable to move to save himself.

Suddenly, Little Red popped out of the hole in Wolf's stomach. "My goodness, you wouldn't believe how dark it was in there." She smiled her sweet smile, dimples showing in her cheeks. Although the stomach slime dampened the effectiveness of her charm somewhat, the woodsman was clearly taken in by it. "Quickly," she said to him, reaching for his wrist to emphasize her point. "You must shoot him."

The woodsman slid his musket from his shoulder, taking steady aim at Wolf's head.

"No, no," Little Red said, pushing against the barrel. "Shoot him in the belly."

The woodsman looked puzzled. "That won't kill him."

"It's not the Wolf she wishes to kill," Grandma said as she pushed her head out of Wolf's stomach.

Little Red froze. Her mouth opened and closed, but no words came out.

"Thank you for your help," Grandma said, smiling to the woodsman as she climbed out of the wolf. "But I must ask you to leave now. We have family business to take care of."

The woodsman glanced from one witch to the other, then nodded and picked up his axe. "I'll be by later to check on you, Grandma, but I wouldn't dream of interfering." He closed the door on his way out.

Grandma stood across from Little Red and held up a lock of golden hair, tightly bound by a single strand of white. "Isn't this the most charming thing?" she asked with a smile. "I just happened to make it while we were both in dear Wolf's stomach."

Little Red stared at the hair, a strange expression of horror on her face. Once she began using her magic to bend others to her will, it had never occurred to her that she might ever have cause to fear.

"Did you think that just because I did not choose to use control, I could not?" Grandma shook her head. "You forgot your early lessons, my dear. Your confidence was your weakness and so you underestimated me. It will not happen again." She tossed the hair into the fire on the hearth, and Little Red vanished in a puff of flame. Then Grandma took her large sewing basket to Wolf's side. "I'm so sorry, my dear. I never dreamed she'd go after you," she said as she threaded a needle. "No, don't try to talk yet. I'll explain what I think you'll want to know, and after you've had a chance to mend, you can ask me anything you like."

She stitched up Wolf's stomach, humming in a way that eased his discomfort. "I'm not sure where my granddaughter learned what she did to rule you, Wolf. If I'd suspected, I never would have asked you to approach her." She tied off the last knot, then helped him to his feet, where he swayed a bit. "And now you must rest," she said, aiding him in the short walk to her bed. She was far stronger than she looked. "It's as well I gave you those herbs before you left," she said as she tucked him under the blankets. "They would have allowed you to shake off a simple spell, and they gave you the power to fight her control."

She insisted that he stay with her until he was healed, giving him all the best food she had. In time, he was as good as new. Feeling that she was ready for a change of scenery, Grandma took the form of a crow and together they went off deeper into the forest where they may still live to this very day.

## *The Kindness of Dragons*

She feared she was the last.

Yarena stared at the large map hanging on the treasure room wall. Far too many of the regions were covered with large black Xs, and when she'd returned last week, she'd had to cross off two more. Her sister's cave in the mountains was empty, and her brother's lair near the sea had been vacant for some time. There was no way to determine if they'd simply moved away or if they'd died. She wondered if dragon slayers, the most foul of all humans, were to blame. She questioned the villagers and forest folk, and grew only more certain that she was one of few, if not the very last dragon. In the local marketplace, she'd heard no new rumors or tales hinting of her kind. The closest she'd come, was the legend spread by her own dear villagers. They talked in hushed whispers of a beautiful woman who lived with a dragon in the nearby hills, sharing in the dragon's wealth, wisdom, and long life. The woman, they said, spoke for the dragon. There had been a time when dragons were so common that everyone knew they were shape changers.

Her hand, human for now, lovingly caressed the leather

cover of a huge book on the marble slab table. It was one volume of many that made up her journals. They spanned centuries, although she'd only started keeping them relatively recently. Much of her youth would have made a dull read. She had little to write about these days, and spent her time reminiscing. To keep her skills from getting rusty, and because people carried such pretty things about, she made sure to pick someone's pockets each time she visited her little village. It was trivial compared to her former exploits. There had been no wars to interrupt. No one needed to be rescued from their wicked parents. Why, she hadn't started a single fight in over a decade, and she used to find them so amusing.

A glint of light caught her attention, and she looked up. Although she hardly moved, her eyes scanned the room. She would have known if the smallest piece of gold were out of place. She inhaled deeply, testing for the scent of an intruder, but there was none. A wall candle flickered, reflecting off a necklace of cut glass. She let out her breath, content that she was just jumping at light ghosts. She removed the necklace from its place and held it up, watching it sparkle as it moved. At the time she'd stolen it, she'd known they weren't the jewels the merchant was trying to hawk them as. She liked all manner of pretty things, valuable or not. Her wizard warrior, Keenan, had often teased her about this weakness. He'd even used it to woo her to him. She'd not had the heart to tell him that she'd been aware of his plans, and that he never would have succeeded if she hadn't been interested to begin with. She and Keenan were a fine team, and she missed both his company and his touch, though nearly a century had passed. Wizard warriors didn't live as long as dragons, no matter what magic she used.

He'd been her last companion, and she'd heard nothing in the last fifty years that could be linked to dragons. She mourned the others. She didn't like being alone. Not even her pretties could distract her, and she often found herself staring at the horrid map.

She froze and sniffed at the air. Someone was coming. She walked swiftly through the caverns of her home. It had been a while since anyone had sought her out, and this one smelled, from the stale hint of ale in his clothes, like a philosopher.

She met him at the front door, propped open to let in the

spring air. He looked as if he couldn't decide whether he should knock or call out. When he saw her, he took a step backward, startled.

Her first impression was that he was very brown. Despite the fact that it was early spring, his face was nearly bronze. His eyes were the same dark liquid color as a deer's. His undyed leather pants and coat were well worn, but not yet shabby. The top few buttons of his jacket were undone, and she could see a bit of a tan tunic beneath. His rich brown hair had been pulled into a tail at the nape of his neck. He carried a walking stick in his left hand and a large pack on his back.

"Hello?" she said. He stared at her in a way that made her check to be sure that she was wearing clothes. She hadn't made the mistake of answering the door naked in four hundred years. As a dragon, clothing wasn't necessary, although she liked to wear pretty things. She was not modest. She thought her human form quite attractive, and saw no need to hide it. She'd once met a troupe of eastern dancers who wore bright sparkly outfits with trailing sheer accents. They were the only garments that really suited her. Today she was dressed in red, with gold and red beads to play off the light.

The young man seemed unable to speak. "May I help you?" she asked.

He swallowed and found his voice. "Oh brave maiden, intercessor for the terrible beast who dwells herein, I beseech thee to grant me wisdom." He lowered himself to one knee and held out his hands, palms up, while resting his staff against his shoulder. His knit gloves were tattered at the edges, and his fingers poked through. Her eyes were drawn to a silver band on his right middle finger. There was a large blue stone recessed into the ring. She wanted it.

"Who are you?" she asked. Keenan had been the last to seek her wisdom, and he hadn't left, even once he'd gained what he sought. They'd traveled the world, causing small mischief where they could and righting wrongs when needed. He'd had a dragon's sense of humor.

"I beg your pardon, great lady," he said. "I'm a humble traveler, a student of the world. I've traveled from a distant land to meet you, who understand the way of the mighty dragon."

She hid a smile behind her hand.  His carefully prepared speech made him sound more naive than he likely was.  "You do realize that wisdom can't be gained overnight, don't you?"

"Uh..."  She'd clearly diverted from his list of expected responses.  "Yes, I understand."

"Wisdom is not an easy thing to attain," she cautioned.  "It can be painful."

He nodded.

"Think carefully before you decide it is truly what you seek."

"I have," he said quickly.  "Even before I left home, and I've had the whole journey to think about it.  Please don't deny me outright.  I've come so far to see you."

She wasn't sure this young man was worthy of the smallest lesson from her, much less a chance at sharing her greater knowledge.  If she sent him away, who knew how long it would be before another came along.  It could be years, and she didn't like that thought at all.  In his favor, he was at least twice as bright as her last few visitors.  Admittedly, knights weren't exactly the smartest people, which was why so few of them returned from their quests.  Most got lost, and it  violated the code of knighthood to ask for directions.  She'd stuffed the last couple glory hunters, and they'd hung on her living room wall until she tired of them.  Then, they'd burned very nicely.

"Please, renowned mistress of truth," he said.  "I will be attentive to your instruction."

"Why have you come to me," she asked, "rather than seeking out a mystic?"  There were so many of them running around these days.  For any belief, there was an available prophet, and most were more than eager to dispense their "wisdom" for a price.  Some were very good at hiding their charges, but a fee was a fee, no matter what pretty name they gave it.

He gave her a very serious look.  "I want genuine wisdom, and such people have little to offer me."

She didn't bother to conceal her amusement.  "Flattery?"

"The truth," he said firmly.  "You've been a hermit longer than any regular mystic."  He smiled and shrugged, then stood up.  "Would you at least consider it, before dismissing me?"

She could sense that he had a strong mind, and she was pleased to note that he wore no religious colors or icons. She found herself liking him, but she wasn't convinced that she should help him. "You have a name, have you not?"

"I'm Daniil." He bowed to her, the movement rehearsed and fluid. "And what may I call you, great mistress of the dragon?"

"Certainly not that," she replied, making a face. "You will call me Yarena. Just Yarena."

His lips twitched as if he were trying not to laugh. "The masters always insisted on proper titles, although none of them were certain how I should address you. Most of them didn't really believe you existed, or that I'd find you."

"Well I do exist, and you've obviously found me." She tossed her head, flipping her red blonde hair over her shoulder. It might be interesting to have a philosopher around for a while. He should at least be able to make intelligent conversation. He might even prove willing in things other than learning. "How long do you plan to stay?"

"As long as necessary," he said. "I'm content to stay until I'm done."

"You're in no hurry to move on?" she asked, wondering if he was sincere. "There's no one waiting for you, *expecting* you?"

He shook his head. "I'm expected nowhere, lady Yarena."

"Just Yarena," she corrected.

He looked embarrassed. "Yarena."

"If you're to be my pupil, you may as well come in and get settled," she suggested, stepping to one side of the doorway and beckoning to him with one finger. "You'll excuse my manners. It's been a while since I've had a house guest."

"I am your humble servant," he said, bowing again.

"You'll have to stop that nonsense," she said. "Respect is fine and good, but groveling turns my stomach."

He smiled and nodded. "It may be difficult to break my training, but I assure you I'll try." He crossed the threshold, then waited for her to lead the way. "I promise to stay out of your way, and the dragon's, of course."

"I doubt you'll be in the way." She closed the door, allowing him time to look around. The little entry made a charming, if slightly cramped, receiving room. Against one wall, there was a small bench, wide enough for two people who were willing to get cozy. A mix of fine dishes, framed paintings, and rolls of fabric was dangerously piled over it. The walls were covered with unusual tapestries. "Give me your jacket," she said. "You won't need it."

"I can see that." He leaned his staff in the corner before easing his gigantic pack to the floor. He handed her his coat, then drew the back of his hand across his upper lip. "Your home is warmer than I'd expected."

"Dragons like heat." She hung the jacket on a brass hook near the door, then reached out to slowly caress his walking stick. "You'll get used to it." Her hand slid up the staff, then back down. "This is lovely," she said, watching him from the corner of her eye. "So smooth, yet so... solid. And this little knob at the top fits so nicely in the hand." She rubbed her palm over that feature in a circular motion, then pointedly met his eyes. "Is it oak?"

He made a funny noise, like a cough and a gasp, and nodded. "White...oak."

"Very nice." She took him through the tunnels in the most direct route to the cave that would be his room. She walked slowly so he could take it all in. She appreciated flashy things and treasure, but she detested filth. Her lair was always dusted and clean, and she kept as many pretties on display as she possibly could.

Daniil looked around his new room, apparently overwhelmed by the accommodations. There was a lot to look at; paintings, jewelry, statues, furniture. "This is really too generous," he said. He barely moved, as if he were afraid he was going to knock something over.

"Of course it isn't," she said. She walked over to the bed, turned back the covers and ran her hand over the sheets as if smoothing out wrinkles. "See? Simple bedding. And it's been getting stale for years. A shame, really." She winked at him. She was certain she'd washed the linens within the last decade. She did a thorough cleaning once every ten years or so. Given the size of her hoard, it wasn't the sort of project she wanted to take on more frequently.

"I assure you, I'll feel like a king." He reluctantly placed his pack beside the dresser.

"It's the smallest alcove in the place," she said, hoping to set him at ease. "Why even the bathing room is bigger." She caught his look of interest. "I'll show you the way. I imagine you'd like to wash up." She could hardly wait to use the spyholes. It had been so long.

"I've been on the road a while," he said with a smile. "I'd hate to track dust through your fine home."

She loved compliments. They were like momentary verbal pretties. "I'll look into dinner while you bathe," she said. "I hadn't planned on company."

"You needn't go through any trouble..."

She cut him off. "It's no trouble." She looked forward to real food again. When she lived alone, she didn't bother to vary her dragon diet, even if it was boring. A change from raw meat, hooves and all, would be welcome. "The bath is this way, and you must let me know if you need any help, any at all."

\* \* \*

"So the king was burned alive in the dragon flame," Yarena said, finishing the story. Daniil sat across from her at the marble table. She had the second volume of her journal open, and, as she'd done every morning for the past few months, she read excerpts aloud to him. She left out the boring details and personal things she wasn't ready to share.

She liked him. They'd had some fabulous discussions, but she still didn't know him well enough. He seemed content to listen to her history and talk about everyday things. She could be patient, and eventually she would understand him better. Time was not a concern.

He looked puzzled after her story about rescuing the princess of Cimeron from her tower prison. Yarena slid a ribbon between the pages, closing the book. "You seem troubled."

"I'm a little confused," he admitted. "There's so little I know about dragons, and the things you've told me haven't made it any more clear."

"What do you need to know?"

He rubbed his chin as he often did when he was thinking. "Well, I guess it would help if I understood dragons better." He shrugged and gave her the self-effacing smile that she was quite fond of. "The legends are inconsistent. I grew up hearing how vicious dragons were. I was also told that they collected treasure, which yours obviously does." He gestured to the room in general. "But some of your old stories mention the kindness of dragons."

She nodded. She'd been aware of the gradual shift in human understanding.

"What you've told me doesn't confirm or deny any of these things," he said. "But I can't comprehend how dragons can be so good and so evil at the same time. I must be missing something important. Something that would make the actions of your dragon more clear."

"So you wish to understand the nature of the dragon?" Yarena asked. She was frankly surprised that he hadn't realized *she* was the dragon and not merely a handmaiden thereof. He wasn't the first to mistake her references of "we" to mean herself *and* the dragon.

"Yes. Well, if you don't mind." He smiled again.

"I don't mind," she said. "You're my student." She set the large book aside as she tried to decide where to start. "Dragons are incredibly long-lived. I've been here, in these caverns, for six and a half centuries." She grinned when that surprised him. "I'm well aware that I don't look my age."

"I knew you'd lived longer than most humans," he said quickly. "But I had no idea..."

She reached over and gently placed one of her hands over the top of his. "Because our time line is different, our perspective and the way we view urgency is affected. Things that seem very important to humans are often trivial to us."

"Then why rescue the princess?" he asked. "Wasn't she trivial?"

She shook her head. "I said they were often trivial, but not always. Occasionally, small events have a way of coming back to bite you." She let her fingertips caress the back of his hand, starting with the webbing between the fingers and moving toward his wrist.

She could feel the thin fragile bones of his hand as her fingers slid back toward his knuckles. "When you throw a stone into the water, you can still see the ripples long after the stone has sunk. It's those ripples we have to watch out for. Sometimes they're larger and more destructive than you'd expect."

"But how do you know which trivial events are going to create dangerous ripples?"

"We can't always know." She twitched her shoulders ever so slightly. "But after a while, we get pretty good at guessing."

"So dragons don't see the future?"

"No. Not in such a detailed or magical sense." They were both silent for a moment. "We get ideas, mostly. Moments of awareness and clarity. Many things move in patterns, and when you live as long as dragons do, you learn to see the patterns."

"And that's how you decide which things to get involved with?" he asked.

She smiled. "Not entirely."

He looked confused. He sandwiched her hand between both of his, stopping the motion of her fingers. "What do you mean?"

"Some events are big enough that we have to get involved," she said. "There are few things worse than a pointless war. War for a good reason is ugly enough, but one with little purpose..." she shook her head. "It's painful to watch such waste for nothing."

"So, a dragon will interrupt a senseless war, or a trivial event with potentially harmful consequences," he summed up.

"And..."

"There's more?" he asked.

"Sometimes we get involved simply because the whim takes us. But this is the generous side of dragons," she said. "And you asked about far more than that."

"I suppose I did." He looked sheepish. "Some of things you've told me seem... well..."

"A bit nasty?" she suggested with a wicked grin. "We can only spend so much of our time being responsible and looking out for everyone else. I'm afraid dragons are possessed of a rather intensely mischievous side."

He stared at her in surprise.

"They're mostly entertainment." She shrugged. "I suspect that tales of ferocious dragons are intended to make us seem far worse than we really are." She met his eyes and dropped her voice to a whisper. "According to many legends, you're in danger of being turned to our wicked ways, simply by being here." She held up his silver ring, which had gotten "misplaced" when he was in the bath. She winked and tucked it into her minimal blouse.

He smiled and reached forward, as if he were going to retrieve the trinket, but diverted his hand at the last minute. "I'm not too concerned."

"Good, because it's not true. Corruption has nothing to do with dragons."

"So there are no bad dragons?" he asked.

She couldn't answer him right away. Although she hadn't left for more than a day here or there, it was beginning to look as though she really was the last dragon. It filled her with a loneliness she'd never felt before. It was one thing to miss the type of companionship Daniil provided, and another altogether to suspect that you were the last of your kind. It made her cold, from the inside out, as if her blood had turned to ice.

"Yarena? Are you all right?" he asked. He firmly patted her hand, then leaned forward on the table. "Is something wrong?"

She shook her head a little, forcing herself to set aside her fear and self pity. "I'm sorry. I got distracted." It took a moment for her to recall what exactly they'd been talking about. "I would never suggest that there are no bad dragons." She tried to recover gracefully. "Some have been truly horrid. Dragons aren't that different from humans." She slipped her hand away from him. "I'm going to lie down. I don't feel well."

\* \* \*

"You know," Daniil said. "I've never asked before, but what *is* that mark?" He had a pile of pillows behind him as he waited for her to join him under the blankets.

She finished brushing her hair and turned to him. "My tattoo?" she asked as she crawled into bed beside him. "It's a dragon. See?"

His fingers gently touched the inside edge of her right breast, where the vibrant green mark had always been. "Are you sure?" he asked. "It doesn't look like a dragon to me. Oh, wait." He kissed the tattoo, fleetingly caressing it with his tongue. "I guess you're right. It is a dragon."

She answered his grin with her own, then she ran her fingers through his hair to the ends. It had been more difficult than she'd expected to coax him into her bed the first time, half a year into his stay. He'd been worried things might get awkward between them, but a year later they were still lovers, and there had been no unpleasantness. His touch was considerate and gentle, and he had the playfulness of a dragon. There was very little that she didn't like about him.

She was concerned that he hadn't realized what she was. She always left that up to the student. She had the odd feeling that he might be keeping a secret from her as well, but she supposed it might just be her own guilty conscience.

She'd given up looking for other dragons for now. The only unmarked regions on the map were far away, and she didn't want to leave Daniil for that long. She didn't think she'd find anything. Besides, when he held her, she wasn't lonely, so it didn't seem terribly important.

"Easy, love. Easy," he whispered.

The room was dark and she realized that she was clinging to him, her fingers digging into the soft skin of his back. She trembled as if she were cold.

"I'm here," he said.

She relaxed as his arms tightened around her. She wasn't alone.

* * *

"Do you realize that you've never mentioned your childhood?" Yarena asked. They were redecorating the large living room again, as she did every solstice. This was the fifth time Daniil had helped, and it went more quickly with a second pair of hands. She had far too many pretties to display at one time, and it was nice to rotate through them.

He finished adjusting the tapestry he'd been hanging, and looked down at her from his place on the ladder. "I guess I didn't

107

think you'd be interested."

"I'd like to know what you did before you came here." She set a recently polished brass and silver lantern on a corner table. The glass panes were beveled, and would reflect the candlelight nicely. "Your homeland is so far away, and I'm curious what you left behind."

He climbed down the ladder more slowly than necessary. "My family didn't approve of the life I chose," he admitted. "They're not terribly big thinkers." He scratched the back of his head, just above the cord that kept his hair bound back. He looked uncomfortable.

"Do you have any siblings?" She'd told him of her brother and sister, although she'd left out the detail that they'd been dragons.

He nodded. "I was one of seven kids."

"Big family," she said, surprised. "What did they expect you to become?"

"A skilled laborer." He placed a large painting in a gilded frame on an out-cropping of rock that served as a natural shelf. "It didn't much matter what trade I took up."

"That kind of life isn't for everyone," she said.

"The life you're born to is the one you're meant to live, or so my mother always said." He shook his head. "Skilled labor had been good enough for our family for generations, and they couldn't understand why I would want anything different. And wisdom doesn't put food on the table." He sat down in a chair and idly toyed with a pair of candlesticks.

"Parents don't always know what's best for their children," she said. "My mother and I often disagreed."

"My family and I rarely agreed on anything," he said, looking at his hands. "We argued. A lot. Just before I started my journey here, we had a really big fight." He locked his fingers together. "My grandfather disowned me."

"Because you sought wisdom?" she asked gently.

"Because I sought you," he said, meeting her eyes at last.

She was stunned. She didn't know what to say. She wanted to tell him she was sorry, but the words got stuck in her throat.

"I wanted you as my teacher," he said. "They hate dragons."

She stared at him for a moment thinking that perhaps he had been hiding something from her after all. "Is there a reason they feel this way?"

He looked down, silent.

"Daniil? What is it?"

"My father was killed by dragons," he said softly.

Dragons didn't typically pursue humans unprovoked. "Had he done something to upset them?"

He nodded. "Oh yes. He deserved to die, and it was right that it happened the way it did." He took a deep breath. "He was a dragon slayer."

She couldn't breathe. The crystal vase that she had forgotten she was holding, slipped from her fingers and smashed on the stone floor.

He jumped to his feet and reached for her hands. "Yarena! Are you all right?"

She took a step backward and yanked her hands out of his reach. "Don't touch me. Don't you ever, ever touch me." She was shaking.

"I'm sorry I didn't tell you," he said, sounding desperate. "I didn't dare. Not at first. I'd hoped you'd judge me as my own person, rather than by my father's misdeeds."

"I took you as my student," she whispered. "I let you live with me. I fell in love with you." That hurt the most.

"Do you think I don't realize that?" His voice cracked on the last word. "Do you think I don't feel the same way?" He stepped closer to her, but she moved back and he stopped. "Yarena, please."

"Monster!" she screamed. She wanted to throw things at him, but she was too angry to pick something up.

"You're not being fair," he said, starting to sound angry. "I didn't choose the family I was born to. I should think that my actions are a better indicator of who I am."

"You never should have come," she said. Instead of looking for others of her kind, she had spent almost three years tricking herself into thinking she wasn't really alone. "You should have known you weren't welcome here."

"You could have fooled me," he snapped

She glared at him. "That's only because you lied to me."

"And that's exactly why I didn't tell you. You would've sent me away without a chance." He was raising his voice now, for the first time since his arrival. "And before you decide that this is all my fault, you've hidden things from me too."

"I don't know what you're talking about," she snarled.

"Short of the tattoo on your breast, I haven't seen any dragons," he said. "If dragons are so wonderful, why haven't you introduced me to yours?"

"You've met the dragon," she said tersely. "All this time and you still haven't recognized me for what I truly am. No human, magic or otherwise, could live as long as I have."

He stared at her.

"I'm not merely a human extension of the dragon. I thought you were bright enough to figure that out on your own. Dragons are shape changers."

He looked appalled, and he didn't seem to be able to speak.

"Now get out of my home."

\* \* \*

The caverns were cold these days, and she didn't bother to do anything about it. She didn't feel the chill so much through her dragon skin, and she rarely wore her human form now. She spent most of her time in the deepest darkest cave, trying to sleep. She broke this pattern to eat, and then, only when she had to. She'd lost a lot of weight in the last four or five months, she wasn't keeping track of time anymore. It didn't matter. Nothing did.

She tried to rally her spirits after she'd sent Daniil away. She resumed her search, but after two months, she returned to her empty home, only to be reminded of him. She could still smell him in certain rooms, and she caught herself wishing he were there. She loved him, and she hated herself for it. He was the spawn of a dragon slayer, and while it wasn't his fault, she couldn't forgive it. Now she was entirely alone, and his father may have had a hand in that. The world was no longer suited to dragons, and in the darkest parts of the night she wondered if despair had killed the rest of her kind.

She gazed at the wall where the badly worn map hung. It

110

was completely covered with Xes now. How had the others vanished so completely without her knowing? She rolled over and turned away. Her tail lashed out and knocked dusty and tarnished goblets across the floor. She didn't care what her pretties looked like. Not even they could make her feel better.

She was roused from her intermittent slumber by a sickening stench. She sneezed twice, scorching the wall opposite her. She sniffed at the air and sneezed again. There was obviously a group of stinking humans outside her home, probably camped on her front lawn. Trespassing. Stupid mangy humans. She hated them all, and there was no way she was going to tolerate them hanging about her home.

She stomped through the tunnels to a cavern that opened upward, like a giant chimney. She launched herself up, soaring past walls of rock. Just when it appeared that she was going to splatter herself on the ceiling, it vanished. She circled a couple of times, stretching her wings. It had been weeks since she'd last flown.

She saw the small group below her. There were nine of them, and they seemed to be waiting for her. She gradually dropped lower, landing between her uninvited guests and her front door. They'd been tampering with the lock. She glared at them.

"I see we have a couple of thieves come to visit," she said, hissing on the sibilants. They smelled even worse up close, which didn't seem possible.

"We aren't thieves," the largest man said. He seemed to be the leader. "We're dragon hunters."

"Dragon hunters?" she demanded. Small jets of flame shot out her nostrils. Although mischievous, she and the others had always tried to help humans along. Some dragons had insisted humans weren't worth the effort, and she was beginning to agree. They forgot too quickly, and they were led astray too easily. "Of all the ungrateful..."

They rushed her then, with inarticulate shouts that she assumed were intended to frighten her while boosting their own confidence. Unexpectedly, one man stayed back, out of the fray. She let out a battle call of her own, shaking the ground, and knocked several down with her tail. With one of her front claws she snatched the sword from the leader's hands. She flipped it over and shoved it through one of his feet and deep into the ground, pinning him to the spot. She turned and spit flame at those who were close. They made a lot of noise at first, but the fire went out fast, leaving them unharmed, if smoking slightly. It gave her a nasty feeling. She looked over the heads of her attackers to eye up the man who'd stayed out of the fight. He was dressed as a trader, but he wore no weapons, which was suspicious in a group such as this. His hands were at his sides, fingers outstretched. Definitely a wizard.

She opened her mouth wide and coughed two fire balls at him. He managed to douse both of them, as well as the ones she threw at each of his companions. She just wanted to kill them and get back to her nap, and she wondered how long it would take to tire him out enough for fire to be an effective weapon. She was going to eat his heart when this was over, the disgusting human.

She grabbed two of the dragon hunters and threw them at the wizard, then torched everything within her range. A couple of the men appeared singed, but that was all. She felt pain across the back of one shoulder and spun to the man who'd slashed her with his sword. She jumped on him, crushing his body beneath her large hind feet. She grabbed his head with both forepaws, and ripped it off with a twist. The dragon hunters were sprayed with blood as she lobbed it at the wizard. Then she bathed the area in fire again.

When the air cleared, they had re-grouped closer to the wizard. His hands were raised overhead as he shouted a spell. She staggered as the sudden drain of energy hit her. It was her turn to be shocked. She recognized the touch of the spell; one no human voice had ever uttered. Somehow, this wizard, whoever he was, had gained access to ancient dragon magic.

She was unable to muster the strength to take to the air. She belched fire at the group one last time before the weakness became too much. She watched in stunned horror as her front claws became hands. He had learned the secret to forcing a shape change. She fell to her knees dizzy and sick. She was the last of the dragons, and now she was going to die. Magic that had once been dragon owned was being used against her. At full strength she might have been able to fight just that. But she had not met them at full strength, and the fight, short though it was, weakened her further.

There was a shout, and she looked up, ready to face death. But her attackers had gathered around their wizard who clutched at a single arrow in his neck. Another man's eye sprouted a matching arrow. Before her enemies could retreat from this new threat, she whispered a spell. She didn't need to be in her dragon shape to work with fire. It took the last of her energy, and she smiled as she fell face forward into the dirt. She saw the dragon hunters burst into flame. As they screamed, the world faded away.

The smoke was still thick when she came to her senses. She'd only been out for a short time. The ground under her face smelled scorched. It was going to be weeks before the grass grew back. She heard footsteps, but couldn't make herself move. Two fingers pressed against her neck, over the pulse. She opened her eyes as she was rolled over. Everything was blurry and unclear. A hand touched her cheek and her face was turned. She blinked a couple of times, and Daniil came into focus. He looked relieved.

"You came back," she mumbled.

"I never left."

She bobbed her head slowly. "Was that you, with the arrows?"

"It was me."

"Thank you."

"I had to." His fingers caressed her cheek. "I still love you, even if you hate me."

"I don't hate you," she whispered. "I've never hated you. Even when I sent you away."

He wrapped her in his cloak and leaned her against him, but didn't try to hold her. "You're thin. Haven't you been eating?"

"Not really," she admitted.

"Yarena, I know things went badly for us," he said. His hand brushed hers, but, rather than clasping, it he merely placed his beside hers. "Do you think maybe we could try again, without any secrets this time? We might be able to get it right."

She nodded.

"I'm sorry I didn't tell you about my father," he whispered.

She shook her head. "You were right, and I'm sorry."

"I am a lot younger than you." He suddenly looked bashful. "You know so much that I don't. I want to be with you Yarena, like we were, only better."

"When you first came to me, I told you wisdom hurt," she looked him in the face. "Do you remember?"

He nodded.

"If we're not to have any secrets, there's something else I need to tell you about wisdom."

He stared at her, almost looking frightened.

"Wisdom can't be given. You can't buy it or steal it. And it's elusive. I would be happy to help you along the way. But if you aren't open to it, if you can't bear the pain of seeing some of your beliefs crushed, you will never have it." She took his hand. "The trick, Daniil, is not to gain wisdom. But to do so without becoming jaded."

## Catch and Release

Arturo brought in the last of his things to find Keevin and Rex already sitting on the floor preparing their snares. It was the first time he'd brought them to his secluded cabin in the Darkest Forest, and they were eager to get to the actual hunting. The Schrellach demons wouldn't be out for a couple hours at the earliest, so they had plenty of time.

Settling himself on the couch, Arturo stretched out his long denim-clad legs in front of him. It had been a tedious drive, despite their early start. The traffic was thick with out-of-province yea-hoos in overlarge vehicles they drove like hot-rods. He crossed his feet at the ankles and admired his new boots for a moment. They'd been expensive, but they were guaranteed not to leak, slip, freeze, melt, explode, or catch on fire. He added a few spells of his own last night, because it was his experience that the people who made hunting gear didn't necessarily know what it was all about. His last pair of boots had dissolved into a gelatinous sludge when he'd been hunting for Radiff Spinning Lizards in the Acid Wash River Region.

Keevin finished his knots and snapped his fingers over the

snare. The loop of rope twitched a little as the enchantment took, and the younger wizard smiled. He started right in on the next one, barely pausing to move the first out of his way.

Arturo had prepared his own things the night before, so he could relax before they went out. He unbuttoned his slightly tattered flannel shirt at the neck. It was nice to be out of his work clothes. The International Bank of Wizards had such a lofty image to uphold, they never had casual days. He waved his hand toward the television on the other side of the room and the screen came to life.

"How's the reception up here?" Rex asked, glancing up.

"Hit or miss," Arturo replied. "Although the programming is pretty bad, so that's not exactly a drawback." They were in the middle of a commercial break, and the advertisement looked poorly homemade. "Some people think it adds to the charm of the Darkest Forest."

The commercial was over. "Crikey! Just look at her!" Exclaimed the young man in olive drab and khaki on the television. He seemed to be over-enunciating, which made him clearly understandable, even to those who might have trouble with an Australian accent. "But just because she's pretty doesn't mean she isn't dangerous."

"Don't you think he's coming off a bit too strong?" Keevin asked. "I mean, how enthused can he really be?"

"Not his fault," Arturo said with a shrug. "Poor fellow's no match for Merlin."

"And there's a man whose a right bloody bastard," Rex said, shaking his head in disgust. "He's too much of a coward to do his own shows, so he sends his poor bewitched werewolf assistant out to do it for him. Pathetic."

Arturo muted the television. He'd watched this episode of *The Basilisk Hunter* with his daughter, who thought Merlin's latest assistant was "dreamy." He liked James the werewolf, for different reasons, and hoped he would last a while, though it didn't seem likely. Merlin was disgustingly commercial, and his last assistant had died in a particularly grisly fashion, on camera of course, while trying to get footage of roc nestlings.

Arturo tugged at his short black braid to make sure the end

was secure.  The last thing he wanted was for his hair to come loose while he was in the middle of the forest.  He'd look much more the stereotypical wizard, but it was very impractical.

Rex placed several wands of varying length and diameter on the low pile carpet in front of him.  He rolled each one over with his fingertips as he sorted them into groups.

Arturo looked over his friend's shoulder to get a better look. "You didn't bring any kill wands, did you?"

"No, I didn't bring any kill wands," he replied sourly.  He was the least conventional of them, keeping his light brown hair cropped close to his scalp and wearing no beard whatsoever.  "But I don't understand what the big deal is."

"You just want a stuffed demon on your ceiling over your cauldron," Arturo said, shaking his head.  "It's revolting.  How would you like to be stuffed and hanging up in someone's house?"

"Who's going to hunt and stuff me?"  Rex chuckled a little at his own question.

"Merlin might," Keevin suggested.

"You're ugly enough someone might mistake you for a talisman to ward off evil spirits," Arturo suggested with a smile.

"Yeah, yeah."  Rex shook his head.  It was an old argument.

"It probably wouldn't be so bad to hunt to kill if you were going to use it," Keevin said.

"Use it?" Rex demanded.  "Schrellach aren't good for much." He looked directly at Arturo.  "I've never seen a spell calling for part of a Schrellach."

Arturo shrugged.  "Claw shavings and hair strands come in handy when working some of the more esoteric protection spells and one of the illusion potions I've got in the family spell-book."

Rex looked surprised.  "You're a disturbed man."  He turned back to Keevin.  "They have no magical use, and I wouldn't eat the meat if I were starving."

"Maybe you should hunt something you would use," Keevin said, "if you want to kill it."  His chin was covered with the soft downy peach fuzz of a beard that was finally starting to come in, and he rubbed at it in a way that suggested that he was unsure how such a comment would be taken.

"You're a radical all right," Arturo said, nudging Keevin with the toe of one boot. The blond man was only a couple decades out of university, and sometimes it was painfully apparent just how young he was. Arturo looked at Rex again. "You don't understand the Schrellach. They're predatory, smart, and absolutely wild. That's a dangerous combination. They have a culture we don't, and can't, fully appreciate."

"You sound like Merlin's assistant." Rex rolled his eyes.

Arturo looked directly at him. "The thrill is in the hunt itself. Killing serves no purpose."

"It culls the herds of the weak," Rex said. "It makes them stronger overall."

"They do that on their own," Arturo said. His family had been coming to the Darkest Forest since he was a child, and he knew a fair bit about Schrellach demons. "Any death we bring them is just waste."

"I'd like a trophy," Rex said. "It'd be nice to go home with something other than just stories, not that those aren't great, but..." He shrugged.

Arturo grinned. "If there's no evidence, no one will know how much you've embellished the tale about the one that got away." He stretched one last time before getting to his feet to start dinner. "Don't worry, you'll get your trophy. It just won't be something you've killed."

\* \* \*

Arturo gave Rex a sharp elbow in the ribs to get his attention. He pointed into the clearing below, where a mother Schrellach was strolling with her two cubs. Their rust colored skin contrasted nicely with the green of the summer forest, but made them tough to spot around dusk. He grabbed Rex by the back of his neck and shook his head when the other wizard appeared ready to go after them. It was one thing to flush an adult, or even a youngling, but it wasn't fair to chase babies, even if they were the only demons they'd seen in the last three days. Not everyone observed the rules, giving all hunters a barbaric bloodthirsty reputation. Arturo was a stickler, which annoyed a lot of folks, but he had his reasons. Lounging in a demon stand was relaxing, but he hadn't come to the forest to relax. He was beginning to wonder if they'd get to experience the chase at all.

The cubs were in a playful mood, pouncing and snarling at each other as they followed their mother. The smaller one jumped onto her brother's back pulling on his stubby red horns as she screeched with delight. He hooted in protest and dropped to all fours spilling her over his head. She rolled away before he could tackle her.

The charming little family hadn't been out of sight more than a few minutes when Keevin came tearing into the clearing. Not far behind him, were two very good sized demons. Their extra long arms reached out periodically in an attempt to grab the young wizard. They were chasing him on two feet, rather than all fours, so he couldn't have irritated them too much. He tripped, rolled forward, and was back on his feet without even stopping. As he neared a tree on the other side of the clearing, he leaped up into the air. An enchanted rope came down within his grasp, and pulled him up into the demon stand across from Rex and Arturo. The two demons jumped up and down beneath Keevin's tree growling and hooting. Schrellach were terrible climbers.

"About time we got some action," Arturo said just before he dropped out of the tree.

His and Rex's arrival distracted the demons, and they lost interest in Keevin. But they weren't stupid and quickly realized they were outnumbered. They crouched down and scrambled out of the clearing, all three wizards close behind. Rex was yodeling, hoping to frighten the beasts into a frenzy. Arturo pulled out a short fat wand and sent harmless explosions of bright light ahead and off to the side, to herd the demons in the direction he wanted. They reached "snare alley," a long narrow clearing densely lined with trees they'd set with snares on the first night. One demon made a misstep and abruptly found his right wrist and ankle bound together. Hobbling, he couldn't keep up with the other Schrellach. Rex and Keevin went after the disabled beast while Arturo continued to chase the one who might yet get away. He had to be careful not to step in any of his own snares, which would make for an entertaining story at his expense. With an explosion of purple and silver sparkles, he startled the demon to veer into the very last snare. He unclipped the rope at his belt, calling on his own skill and the lasso's magic to catch the beast around the shoulders rather than the neck. It worked, and he gave the rope a hard jerk pulling the Schrellach backward. The lasso obediently bound the fallen demon's arms to his sides.

"Nice catch!" Rex called. He and Keevin were dragging their demon over. He was squirming and shaking his head, tossing his tangled black mane.

Arturo's catch was behaving more sedately, as if he knew he was in no real danger. They sat the two beasts side by side and admired them for a moment. Both were young males, strong and healthy, tricked into the chase by Keevin. So much for culling the herds, Arturo thought. "I guess we'd better make the trophies so we can let these fine fellows go."

"You're just eager to get back to the cabin for some beer," Rex said. "Can't we keep them a little longer?"

Arturo shook his head. "The longer we have them, the more danger there is to them, and to us, honestly. Their pack will come looking before too long." He was amused by the surprise on his friends' faces. Most wizards weren't aware that Schrellach lived in groups. "We've had our fun. There's no reason to keep them beyond that."

"You know he's right," Keevin said. "Besides, they'll be even bigger next year."

"And smarter," Arturo said. He dug in his pocket for a moment and pulled out a root. With a small knife he carved the root into a rough image of his Schrellach. Out of the corner of his eye he could see Keevin and Rex doing the same thing. He touched the little poppet to the demon's forehead then cast the spell that turned the root into a scale accurate model of the same demon. Even the skin and horn colors were spot on. Pleased with his trophy, Arturo showed it to the Schrellach before tucking it into the front pocket of his blue and black quilted-flannel shirt.

All three wizards stepped back a good distance before releasing the magic on the ropes holding the demons captive. The one Arturo had caught stood and looked at them for a moment while his companion rushed off into the woods. "So next month, we catch you?" His voice was deep, more of a rumble, and he spoke slowly.

"We'll see," Arturo said. Very few Schrellach spoke wizard language, and fewer still spoke it to wizards.

The demon smiled, showing his large double canine teeth, and nodded before dropping to all fours and disappearing into the forest.

"I didn't know they could talk!" Rex looked as if he felt betrayed.

"Not all of them can, at least not in ways we'd understand," Arturo said, leading the way back to the cabin. "It'll make a nice story back at the office."

"Will it ever!" Keevin slapped Rex on the shoulder. "It's a good thing we let them go, don't you think?"

"I suppose," Rex admitted. "You don't think he really meant it, do you? That he'll catch us next month?"

Arturo shrugged. "Could happen. I told you they were predators."

"You don't think they'd want to eat us, do you?" Rex asked.

"Well you *were* wondering who'd want to stuff you," Keevin reminded him.

Arturo shrugged again. "That's just one of the reasons I don't kill. It's not the kind of reputation I want to have if the tables get turned."

www.ingramcontent.com/pod-product-compliance
Lightning Source LLC
Chambersburg PA
CBHW031837170626
46807CB00004B/1497